ROUGH RETURN

SCREAMING DEMONS MC
BOOK FOUR

SUMMER COOPER

SIENNA CHANCE

LOVY BOOKS

Lovy Books Ltd
20-22 Wenlock Road
London N1 7GU

Cover by SC Creative

PROLOGUE

Fiona Strong was a genius. A woman out to get her man. She snapped the bustier, took a drink from her pilfered flask of vodka, and pushed her boobs up. Cleavage never hurt anyone and this thing gave it to her en masse. The overhead fluorescent lighting wouldn't do much for her pale skin tone - might even make her look a little pastier than a usual redhead even - but she'd chosen the outfit knowing the mall wasn't much for mood lighting.

For seven years, she'd done every damned thing she could think of to get Grier's attention, from makeovers to not-so-subtle hints to standing beside his bike while she sucked a lollipop. She'd seen that one on a movie and the hero had practically had to stop, drop, and roll before he carried the heroine to bed. But Grier had shooed Fiona away like she had some sort of communicable disease. And for seven years, not so much as a kiss had passed between them.

Well, not today, cowboy. Today, Grier would see Fiona — and a lot more of her than her shorts and tank tops allowed him. And with a little luck, he'd feel her, too. Otherwise, convincing Daddy to make him take his twenty-year-old daughter shopping for clothes that wouldn't fit in her closet was all for nothing.

She popped open the dressing room door and stepped out. Grier sat on a bench, elbows on his knees, blond head down, eyes on his phone. If she focused on his pretty face, she would lose the benefit of her Grey Goose courage, so she watched his hands instead. Long, semi-calloused fingers. She stood for a second imagining the delicious friction they would cause against her skin. A man like Grier knew passion, knew exactly how to bring a woman to the brink and he would. Even if it was her first time. Then he would send her shooting over the edge to real womanhood.

Focus, Fi.

She lowered her voice and waited until he glanced up to swipe her tongue over her paradise-pink painted lower lip. "What do you think?" She turned to the side and leaned against the door frame, not as much for support as because she knew from hours spent alone with a mirror that her curves played better at an angle. Grier needed to see and appreciate the full effect.

He looked down at his phone. "No."

What the hell did that mean? "No, what?"

"It means no. No, I'm not going to let Max kill me because I let you buy that." He lifted his chin again then turned it back down. "Now go change."

He might have thought she missed the color in his cheeks, the way his grassy green eyes went dark and dangerous, but she didn't. She also didn't miss his cocked eyebrow to her non-reaction. In a planned response to his planned command, she pushed her boobs higher, gave a shoulder shimmy that would have caused a wardrobe malfunction if she'd thought to get the bustier one size smaller, then turned to head back through the louvered door.

The bustier was the least revealing of all the garments— okay, lingerie— she'd chosen to try on. Of course, before she walked out in one of the teddies or sheer camis, she'd need a few more shots from her flask.

Let the games begin.

* * *

Down boy. Dear God. If Max knew half the shit going on in Grier's head, he'd not just kill him. He'd kill him slowly, take a piece at a time to toss up and down the east coast. *You touch her, I'll kill you.* Grier looked down at his dick. It twitched with need. "Stop it."

Truth told, this whole thing—impure thoughts and half-hard cock—was all Max's fault. If he hadn't forced Grier into babysitting Fiona while she tried on every provocative garment housed in the Prudential Center Mall, he would've been out riding with Kye, protecting the club's interests instead of imagining the old man's daughter naked and writhing underneath him.

He closed his eyes and counted to ten, then shifted in his seat to relieve some of the below-the-belt pressure threatening to make him sterile before his time, but it didn't work. His dick still throbbed against his zipper. And when Fiona opened the dressing room door again, any blood left in his brain shot straight south of his equator.

Holy shit. Sheer. Black. A satin robe. Miles of leg covered in fishnets and secured by a red and black garter. With bows. Fucking bows. And the cleavage. She turned a slow circle and the robe flared, also did nothing to cover the thin line of fabric between two luscious ass cheeks. She opened the robe in front, and his tongue rolled back in his head. Her nipples poked the fabric into points he wanted to put his mouth around. And by wanted, he meant… *really* wanted.

Sheer wasn't the right word. Transparent. See-through. Fucking fabulous.

He coughed, choked, lost any breath he might have been able to draw, then stood and held his leather jacket in front of her. If anyone saw her dressed like this, Max would heat a steel pipe and poke his eyes out. Grier forced her back into the dressing room.

And it wasn't until she shoved him onto a small chair inside and straddled his lap that he realized his mistake.

She ground her hips against his cock as she latched her lips onto his throat. He should have stood and pushed her away but each delicious swirl of her tongue and every pull of his skin as she sucked the vein just below his jaw went straight to his dick. Coherent thought took a minute to break through the haze of want and need and desire so thick he groaned.

"Stop, Fi…o…na."

She guided his hand to her left breast. Her perfect left breast, which probably matched her perfect right breast. The thought didn't play well with his good intentions, and he closed his eyes as she used her hand to swirl his over a pert and already pebbled nipple. He snapped his jaw shut to keep another moan tucked in his throat.

Too many more of those hip rotations and he'd lose his fucking mind. She dragged her mouth up his throat to his ear. Breath hot, she whispered, "Take me, Grier. I want you to be my first."

His brain, rather the mush she'd left behind, finally joined the party. He stood, and she slid down his body, making the space that should have been between them irrelevant. The robe pooled at her feet and she slipped the straps of the nightie down her arm so that it fell to join the robe.

Oh, dear God. Max would kill him.

Rather than reach out and haul her against him the way he wanted to, he exhaled from deep in his gut and walked out.

1

The plane lurched, and Fiona's fingers curled around the armrests, her white knuckles the only indication of her sheer terror. She breathed out slow and glared at the sleeping man in the seat next to hers. The traitor. The only reason she would die if the plane plummeted from the sky. Grier fucking Owen.

And wasn't it just some bullshit karmic justice that island life agreed with him? Made him prettier than before. Yeah. She could admit it. To herself and no one else, but admit it, anyway. He'd always been gorgeous. Now, though, blonder. Tanner. More muscular. Probably even taller.

It didn't matter. She owned him now. Or she would once Max - and boy, did he hate when she called him that instead of *Daddy* - finally quit hanging onto a life that didn't want him anymore. The thought caused an ache in her chest.

He'd been *Daddy* when she was a little girl. And despite the tough-guy tattoos and dirt under his fingernails, he'd attended every tea party and teddy bear wedding. When she was a teenager, he became *Dad*—the father who taught her how to ride and fix cars, who'd scared away every guy she'd ever been interested in and had made Grier her official babysitter. Most recently, he'd become *Max*, the man whose empire would become hers if she could keep Bruce, Frank or Nate from claiming it for himself, if she took everything Max taught her and put it to use.

He'd sent her to Belize to bring back the traitors—Kye and Grier—and the bitch who'd turned Kye, Eliana something. They'd bought an island. Tried to hide from Screaming Demons motorcycle club, her club. Well, her father's club. And it was time for their restitution to be paid.

But being in Belize, chatting with the locals, she'd heard one name over and over—Grier. Grier learned to surf. And build things. Bring smiles and kindness to the little kiddies who worked the markets and played in the streets. Grier. Grier. Grier. Something inside of her snapped, stabbed her inside. Grier fucking Owen. Made her weak. Made her want. Thinking back over all the years she'd tried to seduce him and failed made her blood boil. She was also annoyed with herself when she thought about how she'd almost begged him to take her to bed that stormy night when they finally came face to face again in Belize. Well, not anymore. She didn't want to let him see how weak he made her.

Of course, she wanted him, but that wasn't the reason she'd brought him back. She brought him back because she needed him. And, okay, she might have had a little revenge on her mind. Not a concrete plan. But a desire to form one.

He opened one eye and looked at her. "See anything you like?"

"No." Of course, he'd catch her staring at him. Damn the karma. After being so adamant that he wouldn't have sex with her in Belize, she wasn't sure what made him change his tone like this, but she wasn't going to let it weaken her resolve - she needed to keep focused on the bigger picture.

"Well, you've changed your tune. You couldn't wait to get your hands on me the other night." He smiled a knowing smile and Fiona started feeling weak again.

"I have a job that I need to get done - that's all."

After a shrug, he shifted in his seat, closer, and Fiona caught a big whiff of him - sunshine and ocean. A couple of days in Pine Hill would cure that. And not that she'd admit it, but she might miss it. She leaned in and breathed deep.

"Did you just sniff me?"

Her skin heated. "No." But oh, God.

"Yes, you did."

"Don't be an idiot." And she might have been talking to herself. What his smile did to her - sweaty palms, racing heart, a dampness in places that should have been dry - meant nothing. A lot of men had that effect on her. None she could think of with Grier so close. "I didn't sniff you. I sniffed the air. Something in your vicinity stinks. I thought maybe you forgot how to shower while you were away."

He chuckled. Deep. Low. Straight to her panties. "On the contrary. Kye and I built an outdoor shower at my bungalow." He shook his head and more of his scent wafted her way. "God, I'm gonna miss that thing."

Picturing him naked didn't help her pulse slow. And the voice did… things. Made her mouth go dry and everything else break into a sweat. She fanned herself with a sky-shopping brochure from the pouch in the back of the seat in front of her. "Your fun in the sun days are over."

He moved away and sighed. "Max part out my bike?"

Normally the guys would have burned it or stripped it out leaving nothing but a frame, but she'd asked for the bike. She had one of her own, but more often than not, she drove her car. Two bikes, one car and only one ass. The math equaled overkill. Actually, keeping his bike made her the kind of pathetic she didn't want to think about. Or acknowledge. Or accept.

"Yeah."

He nodded. "I figured." And his wistful tone absolutely didn't affect her.

"It's what happens when you betray your club." She narrowed her eyes, hanging onto the anger, to the loyalty to the club. Grier had chosen Kye over everything he'd vowed to protect, over every guy who'd had his back, every brother who would have given their life for his, and over the woman, Fiona, who would have given him everything.

For Kye. A "friend" who hadn't lifted one damned finger to stop her from dragging Grier back to face Max. And considering what Max could order done to him, Kye wasn't a very good friend.

"He put a hit on Kye and Eliana."

Not a secret or an excuse. "On another traitor and his girl. That's how things work. You knew it going in. Club before anything. Kye forgot that because of his woman. I don't know what made you forget it."

Grier scoffed. "My loyalty was to the club. Not your dad."

"My dad is the club."

"And he's dying."

Her heart thudded to her stomach. She didn't need this bastard to read the future. She was the one holding

Max's hand every night, praying he would get through just one more day, not knowing how to let go. She turned toward the window. "Fuck you, Grier."

Maybe, just maybe, when she was in charge, she'd make Grier eat those words and every other he'd ever spoken. Along with a few of his teeth.

"I'm sorry about your dad."

She didn't answer. In truth, she couldn't. The lump in her throat—the one for the little girl losing her daddy—wouldn't let her.

GRIER FIRMED UP HIS RESOLVE—OR rather, resignation—to his fate. Well, not quite. Knowing what Max would do to him, actually would order done, made resignation an optimistic idea. At least when it was over, he'd be free. Not free as much as dead. A kind of free, maybe.

And without getting laid one last time. Maybe he should have taken Fiona to bed in Belize when she'd first demanded it, because unless she could stop hating him long enough to join the mile-high club with him, his luck twisted from good to bad. And the chance of her letting him stop off to pick up a woman for a quickie ranged from slim to never-gonna-happen. So, death was coming. More accurately, he was jetting toward it at about six-hundred miles per hour.

He shook off the thought. No point in dwelling. Instead, he watched Fiona. Stared at her. Two years had knocked the innocence off. Turned her into a woman. She kept her long red hair down now, and soft curls framed her face, making her stormy eyes all the angrier. Maybe from dealing with her father dying or maybe she'd finally discovered the kind of bastard her father really was. No matter the reason, the differences didn't end with her hair. She carried herself with confidence now. Not that she wasn't a fireball of arrogance before, but this was different. More controlled. More real. And what could he say about the courage she'd used to come to Belize without backup and with no guarantee Kye wouldn't shoot first and dispose of the body later? He hadn't wanted to let Kye and Eliana see how he felt about her when they'd first met Fiona, but she would have been the perfect woman for him had she not been so intent on killing him.

And her face, the features once soft and innocent, had hardened, grown wary. Still beautiful. And he would never tell her. Would take to his grave how hot she looked. How much she affected him, always had. Even when it was wrong. And when she'd lifted her chin, daring Kye to shoot her, his body reacted in ways he couldn't afford to think about. Not if he wanted to maintain any pride.

He'd never quite forgotten that day at the mall, the

way she'd looked and tasted… how her body fit with his. Never would he tell her the memory that those few minutes in the dressing room had been the jump start to some long, lonely nights full of dreams of her.

She hadn't changed perfumes either—still smelled of flowers and something sweet he'd never quite been able to identify. But there were flowers in Belize—exotic with white and orange blossoms—that smelled like her, made his thoughts head straight for the little box he'd put her in when he left. Made him remember holding her against him.

He shifted, his dick straining against his jeans, and the move brought him closer to her which was counter-productive to his objective.

When he bumped her shoulder, she turned a glare on him. "What are you doing?"

He cleared his throat. "Um, just… looking out the window." Lame.

"Thinking about jumping?" Ah. So her smug smile had the same air of self-satisfaction he remembered. "Smashing your face against the pavement at a thousand miles an hour is probably kinder than what Max has planned for you."

"Probably true." But escape by parachute could work. Escape back to Belize. Of course, it would mean leaving Fiona behind, but that was okay. He'd done it before.

2

Fiona breathed deep. Her dad was going to be five kinds of pissed off with an extra dose of homicidal rage that she'd left Kye and his woman on the island. Grier had come along quietly, either incredibly brave or, more likely, unbelievably stupid. Especially since he didn't know that Max handed down the order to have Grier ended. He would have guessed, of course, but not known for sure. Her father's unpredictability made sure of it. But he wouldn't know Fiona had swooped in and saved him. He would be indebted. She would own him. Until she got what she wanted, what Max wanted her to have, and she tired of him, at least.

She glanced over as the hired car sped toward her childhood home. If Grier was nervous, he kept it hidden behind his closed eyes and half-smile. She gave him a semi-gentle shove. "How can you sleep?" She really wanted to know.

"I'm not sleeping. I'm resting." His eyes came open, only half-way, the sleepy eyes that turned her stomach to mush and had her imagining how he'd look after a couple of solid rounds in her bedroom.

"Okay. How can you rest?"

"What should I be doing? Wringing my hands? Clutching my pearls?" He shrugged and it made her want to rethink her most recent decisions. "I've always known Max knew where we were. And I've always known he would come." He grinned, and she ignored the warmth that started in her belly and spread lower. "I've packed some living into these last few years."

"Two years of getting laid by pretty island girls going to make the dying easier?" God, he was stupid.

He shrugged. "I would've never thought he'd send you."

"I volunteered." True. Max had wanted to send Bruce and Frank, but Fiona convinced him that if the guys went, Kye and Grier would never make it to the plane.

"Miss me, did you?"

Oh sure. With nothing to lose, she'd assured him he only had hours left to live and he decided to be the flirt she'd wanted him to be two years ago. She looked out the window.

"I think about that day at the mall sometimes." His

voice, soft, deep, went straight through her. "Max would have killed me."

"He's going to kill you now."

Grier nodded. "I know. And I felt so chivalrous back then, but hindsight and all…I should've just slept with you." The leather groaned as he twisted his body. "We've got time. Still up for it?"

"That's your best line, dead man walking?" She clucked her tongue. "It's a wonder you're not dying a virgin. I was young then - I'm not so stupid now." But the image in her head probably shot steam out her ears.

Was that regret in his eyes? God, she hoped so.

He shook his head. "Wow. You can really hold a grudge, huh?" And somehow, he'd managed to lace his fingers through hers, and stroked the inside of her wrist with the index finger of his free hand. "What if I said I was sorry?"

"Max will probably appreciate it. He'll still kill you, but he likes a good apology." And if anyone would know, it was his daughter.

"I don't care about apologizing to Max." He looked down. "I meant, I wanted to say I was sorry to you. I never stopped thinking about you."

She pretended to think on it because her heart in her throat wouldn't let sound or breath escape around it. She exhaled slowly. "I guess I would immediately tell the driver to turn around and take you straight back to the airport. Of course."

He smiled, that damned finger still drawing little circles on her arm. "Sarcasm?"

"What do you think?" She yanked her wrist away as the car pulled in front of Max's house. If only Grier knew how long and often she'd wished for him to say something like that in his soft, husky voice, he wouldn't have teased her. Probably he was just toying with her, trying to save his own pathetic ass from the beatdown he deserved.

Simple bastard.

And while she hadn't really worked out much of a plan beyond keeping him alive, she'd let him cool his heels for a while, wonder what sorts of torture his future, the one she'd made sure he had, would bring.

It wasn't much of a plan, but it would do for now.

GRIER HAD BEEN to the house where Fiona grew up several times. Back then, the siding had been white and the shutters black, and the porch surrounded by land-scaping Grier had spent many an hour weeding.

Sometime in the last two years, the siding had been replaced with light brick, and the shutters by fancy white trim. Shrubbery and stone steps took the place of the porch where Fiona had tried to kiss him when she was fifteen and he was twenty-one.

"Place has changed."

"A lot's changed since you turned traitor." She stomped up the steps ahead of him.

"Fiona, wait." He held onto her arm figuring she would pull away, but she stood, skin warm under his hand, pulse point in her throat quietly throbbing. He needed to get his brain out of his pants. Warm skin and throbbing hearts weren't nearly as important as making her understand. "Kye was the only family I ever had." She would never agree to help him escape, if an opportunity even presented itself, unless he could make her see why he'd risked everything to help Kye. "You had Max. You were always someone's everything. Kye and I grew up without anyone in a system that didn't give a shit. This club is about loyalty and having each other's backs, but when your dad put out that hit on Kye, no one spoke up. They just followed because it was Max. And you know he wasn't playing straight about Kye. Or Eliana."

"I don't know anything of the sort." But her eyes betrayed her words. And Grier had hope.

"Kye needed me. And I would do it again." She didn't blink, but she didn't move when he transferred his hand from her arm to cup her cheek. "I would've done the same thing for you."

This was his last chance to convince her, to swing her around to his side if that was even possible. He leaned in, close enough to see every fleck of silver in her gray eyes, to smell her perfume, to feel her slow breath on his lips. She jerked away, and his stomach lurched. He'd over-estimated her attraction to him. Two years ago, one crook of his finger would have brought her running. Now all she could do was glare.

He sighed. "Take me in."

She opened her mouth, slapped it shut, and turned to lead him through the front door. And while the outside of the house had changed, the living room wasn't even recognizable. A hospital bed blockaded the stone fireplace. Tables and lamps, family memorabilia and bric-a-brac had been taken away in favor of monitors and machines, medicine bottles and a woman whose short white skirt said she was either a nurse subject to a dress-code likely demanded by Max, or she was an on-call stripper who happened to know how to stick someone with an IV needle. Pictures of Fiona, a documentation of her school life from kindergarten through high school, still hung on the wall along with a big-screen TV.

Hamilton moved from his spot in the corner. *Oh, shit.*

In the last two years, the already formidable man at arms had packed on the muscle, and obviously not upped his shirt size. Bulges and ripples strained against the tight black fabric. His step quickened.

This was going to be bad, but fuck if he'd flinch. Or blink. Or beg for mercy.

He glanced at Fiona. One last look. Light cast a halo at the crown of her fiery red hair and if Max hadn't groaned, Grier would have seen the fist coming for him. He would have ducked, blocked, maybe managed a side-step. What he wouldn't have done was take that hit full on the jaw. He also wouldn't have landed on his back next to the bed. And maybe not seen stars.

As Hamilton stood over him, Grier considered his options. Crawl away? Get up, and maybe by tomorrow be able to run. Or take it. Hamilton yanked him up, steadied Grier with one hand and doubled him over with another swing to his gut.

Grier's breath whooshed out, and it took a few long seconds before he could catch another. "Fuck, Ham." He coughed, sure that if he dared look, there would be blood.

A soft "That's enough" followed by an even quieter "For now" came from the bed.

Grier struggled to straighten. Probably had a broken rib. He ignored his pain and focused on the man who'd once trusted him with his most prized possession, Fiona. Not so long ago, Max had been larger than life. Tough. Feared. Respected. Even revered. Now, his body had gone rogue, fighting itself from the inside so that the outside appeared frail and small.

Wires and tubes poked out from beneath the pile of blankets covering him, and a bag of piss that needed draining dangled from a tube clipped to the bedframe.

A tight pain ached in Grier's chest, only in part due to Hamilton.

"Leave us." Max pushed a button and the head of the bed raised him to a sitting position. He looked more like himself, stern, angry, ready to dole out orders. He looked past Grier to Hamilton. "Take her home."

Hamilton nodded, but Fiona's eyes narrowed. Grier might have asked her to stay - defying Max didn't seem to be much of an issue now - but the side of his face throbbed. When he lifted his hand to touch his cheek, it came away sticky with blood.

Fiona stared at her father. "I'll wait outside but I'm not leaving him here alone with you." She pushed past Grier to stand next to her father's bed. "I don't trust the son of a bitch."

Max chuckled. "It'll take more than a pussy like Grier to do me in, baby." He covered her hand on the rail with his. "Go on home and relax. I'll see you in the morning."

She kissed his cheek then turned to Grier. "I'll be waiting outside. You try escaping and Hamilton is gonna finish you off. Clear?" Grier nodded, and she glanced back at her father. "Don't wear yourself out, Daddy, okay?"

It would have been a touching moment if not for the pain radiating through Grier's entire body. Visions of an agonizing death flashed through his mind. Didn't take a genius to figure out this wasn't going to be a good day.

Max waited until the door latch clicked behind her and they were alone before he spoke. "I want to make you a deal."

"Okay." Deals with Max only ever benefited Max, but unless he could figure an escape plan that didn't end with his face at the end of Hamilton's boot, he didn't have another choice.

"I want you…" He breathed out slowly then dissolved into a coughing fit. His chest rattled, and his face faded to an almost ghostly white, but he held up a hand to stop the nurse from injecting medicine into his IV tube. "I want you to marry Fiona." He closed his eyes even as Grier's brain screamed at him to object. Loudly. "Take over for me."

"Max, no. You're gonna…" Pull through? Not likely. "Max, she'll never agree."

"She will."

"I betrayed you." Plus, he had no intention of marrying anyone. Ever. No matter how badly he wanted to taste her skin, feel her hair brush over his chest, touch her in ways he'd only ever dreamed of.

"I'll call off the contract."

"Max…" Marry Fiona. Take over for Max. Insanity. Pure and simple insanity. "She'll never…"

"If you don't marry her, I'm going to double the price on your head."

This had to be a joke. "Does she even know?"

"She knows this all belongs to her. But she's young and reckless. The boys will need time to learn to follow her." He gasped and covered his face with an oxygen mask. Grier waited, his mind spinning, his guts in his throat. "You can help her. She needs you."

Oh, the flawed logic. Of course, it was probably the only thing keeping him alive. "What makes you think anyone, her or them, will listen to me?" He should've kept his mouth shut and agreed, let the old man die thinking he would care for Fiona, then escape. But maybe his mouth knew something his brain didn't.

"They'll follow you because Hamilton will follow you. He gave me his word. And his word means some-thing." He tossed the oxygen mask to the side and pulled himself higher in the bed. This was the Max he knew. Calculating. Smart. Always with some plan. "Since you first came around, asking to be a demon, I knew you had something. And she saw it too. Pined over you when you ran out. She'll do this."

Grier had an aching jaw that said Hamilton wasn't

completely on board with the follow-Grier plan. "Why not just have Hamilton marry her?"

Max coughed again and held his chest before he shook his head. "Because I don't want ugly grandchildren."

Fair point. Hamilton was a beast. Over-sized. Crooked nose. Buck-teeth. He'd always reminded Grier of a gargoyle. And even Fiona's beauty wouldn't offset the damage Hamilton's genetics would inflict on the family tree. But no fucking way was that Grier's problem. And not much chance Max would live long enough to see grandchildren.

"Max…"

"Marry her or Hamilton is going to finish you off. You have until tomorrow to decide. Now get out."

Just as he'd suspected. Today was not a good day.

3

Fiona didn't want to marry Grier. She wanted to screw him and screw him over then send him back to his little island.

"It's the only way Bruce won't take over the club, Fi." Hamilton handed her a beer then folded his body to sit next to her. "If you don't marry Grier, Max is gonna have to name Bruce as his successor."

"It's bullshit." But true. Man's world. Man's rules. And no way any of those hard-ass bikers would follow her. Not without a man beside her. And Grier, a weak traitor she could control through Hamilton, was at least easy on the eyes. And if not Grier, she could end up with Nate or One-eye Jim. Neither of whom had been chosen as Demons because of their good looks or sparkling personalities.

Hamilton looked at her and smiled. It transformed

his entire face. Gone were the hard lines and usual scowl, replaced by a softness he saved for her. "It's what Max wants." He squeezed her shoulder. "Dying wish and all."

Oh, not fair. "I know."

"So, the way I figure, you marry the traitor, punish him every day until Max dies, get the boys on your side, then divorce him, and I'll make him disappear." His grin spread across his face. "You know how much I want to make him disappear."

She laughed for a second because he expected her to hate Grier, which she did, but maybe not as much as she should. "Yeah, but who's going to want him riding with them? The only thing we can trust him to do is tuck his dick between his legs and run."

Hamilton nodded. "Why'd you agree to bring him back then?"

Good question. Even better question after Hamilton filled her in on Max's plans for her future. Plans she had to pretend not to know and not to be the mastermind behind.

The door behind her opened and closed. And thank God because Hamilton asked a question she'd rather die than answer.

She didn't bother turning around. It could only have been Grier. "Because she missed me. Obviously."

She rolled her eyes at Hamilton. "I like your face

better now that Ham started rearranging it. It's a good look. We'll call it *punch of the day*."

"I don't know, babe. Think of the wedding pictures."

The word *babe* didn't affect her. Absolutely not. And her hands shaking had nothing to do with him sitting beside her either.

He took her beer and pressed the bottle to his bruised cheek. "Is this the craziest thing you've ever heard?" He'd asked Hamilton who stood and walked away. "I'm not really feeling the love." He chuckled and the sound settled in her belly. Low in her belly. "Max is losing it, right? And we're humoring him?"

Fiona didn't look at Grier. Couldn't. "He's serious. Ham said he told him to tell the guys you're back and your absence will be explained when they need to know. So, he can pull this plug anytime he wants." All true. All too ridiculous to fall into place this easily, but Grier, sitting beside her said it was working.

"And you're willing to go along? Not wait to marry someone you love?"

Oh, shit. Someone you love. Did he have that someone waiting for him in Belize, some island babe he'd rather spend his life with? She'd never considered he might have someone waiting for him to get his Pine Hill shit worked out.

"I don't have a choice." Neither did he, island honey or not.

"You could have given me a heads up." He finished her beer then rolled the bottle between his palms.

"Ham just gave you all the heads-up you're getting."

He sighed. "Fiona, we don't really know each other. And even if we tie the knot, the club is never going to accept me."

His excuses not to marry her were really starting to piss her off. She hardened her voice and squelched the little one in her head that begged her to try to see his point. Consider his feelings. Gibberish.

"They'll do what I tell them to do." Which meant they would do what she told Hamilton to tell them to do.

"So, just curious, but is this your way of getting me into bed? Because all you had to do was ask." What she wouldn't have done to wipe that smug smile off his face once and for all. "Go on. Ask me."

Not again. Not ever. He would do the asking. The begging. One way or the other.

"Seeing me married, even if it's to you, is my father's dying wish."

"How dutiful of you."

Oh, for hell's sake. She'd had enough. "Listen, I don't give two shits what you do. Marry me or don't. It's not me they're all going to come after. And all of those other guys would be happy to hop into my bed with their ring on my finger."

She was almost to the car when she heard his soft,

"Okay." And if her heart beat a little faster and her knees went a little bit weak, she'd blame low blood sugar any day of the week over giving Grier that kind of credit.

GRIER SAT beside Fiona as she drove him to the clubhouse. She'd hidden her eyes behind a pair of Ray-Bans, and he couldn't read her expression from just the hard line of her jaw. He watched her anyway, memorized every move and detail—the careless dangle of her wrist over the steering wheel, the glints of black and white blonde woven through her luscious red hair, the way her shirt stretched tight over her chest.

So much about her had changed, but nothing more so than the loss of innocence and the hero worship he'd always seen in her eyes when he pulled up on his bike.

On the island, he hadn't missed his bike. The sun, sand, and surf had been enough to keep him content. But being back in Pine Hill, smelling the exhaust fumes bouncing off the pavement, he ached to ride, to feel the roar of the engine, to command it and feel it respond to every flick of his wrist or flex of his thigh. No bike would ever replace his '71 Super Glide, the bike he'd spent months restoring with Max and Kye. That she'd been destroyed made his guts clench.

He went back to watching Fiona. Thinking about the

bike hurt too much. She turned onto Hell Hollow Road. It narrowed in that old familiar way, and she maneuvered around the curves like she'd taken her driving lessons from NASCAR.

She crossed the tracks that used to carry steel in and out when this had been a warehouse for the long-ago closed steel mill. The club had converted the warehouse to its center of business and pleasure.

"Did you bring me here so they can kill me?" He was only half-kidding.

"No one's going to touch you, you big baby." He didn't move. He honestly hadn't thought he'd ever see this place again, but the building loomed in front of him like a memory he couldn't decide was good or bad. "Never knew you to be such a chickenshit, Grier."

But she had it all wrong. He wasn't afraid. He was savoring the sight of it all. Of home. The only place he'd ever felt he belonged.

He sighed and popped open the door. "Lead on, Princess." She cringed at the little pet name, but kept walking then yanked the door open. All he could see inside was darkness. An ominous absence of light. Or maybe it just seemed that way.

When he inched through the door, he saw plenty. And not much had changed. The TVs were bigger, sofas older, the floor more scuffed. But the bar still had a liquor shelf fit for a swanky nightclub, a who's who of hard liquor. The gym's sweat sock and vodka smell still permeated every other space, and the old chains and gear racks hung from the ceiling as a permanent reminder of what had once been.

A couple of new guys, hardened criminals judging by their prison tattooed faces, sat with Bruce and Frank at one of the poker tables. Bruce had five stacks of chips, a card in his lap, and the best poker face in the club. Grier didn't mention his penchant for cheating. No one had told him. He'd learned the expensive way. Looked like the new guys would, too.

One-eye Jim had a Hell Kat on his lap on one of the sofas, and Jez, queen Hell Kat, shot him a smile as she handed Nate a beer at the bar.

No one moved. No one breathed. Not until Fiona laced her right hand with his and held up her left, the one with a boulder-sized diamond on her third finger.

"Holy shit." As soon as the words left his mouth, Fiona dug her fingernails into his skin. Probably would have reached bone had he not jerked. She eased her hold.

Grier waited, hands stinging, jaw pounding, stomach revolting. And he had questions. Like where the hell did she get that thing? Also, did she expect him to pay for it?

A slow throb started at the base of his skull and migrated to his forehead, and still, no one moved. No one but Fiona, who used their clasped hands to wrap his arm around her waist, as she laid her free hand over his heart. She pressed in close, intoxicating, suffocating, and so damned sexy his dick turned to stone.

When she pulled his head down to press her lips to his ear, he groaned. "Play along." Her whisper warmed his ear and every cell to his toes.

He nodded because, even if he wanted to answer, there wasn't enough blood left in his brain for natural thought to occur.

She was not so afflicted. Of course, her breasts weren't rubbing along her forearm with each inhale and exhale she took. "All right. I know what you all think you know. But Grier didn't run out with Kye. He was on club business abroad, protecting that attorney and making sure she knew our business needed to remain private."

Grier didn't widen his eyes or drop open his mouth. Instead, he kept his jaw clenched and his face blank. Wasn't she just full of surprises?

Frank stood. "Bullshit. I was here when he ran off. Max was ready to kill him then, and I'd bet my dick he still wants him dead."

Fiona hardened her voice. "Lucky for you, I'm not in the mood to add to my collection of tiny cocks."

One-eye pushed his Hell Kat away and stood, his eyes burning with anger. "Why should we believe you?"

Grier had a choice. Stand up for "his woman" or walk away a coward. "Because she said it."

"She says a lot of things." His hand rested on a knife sheathed at his belt. "Doesn't make them true, and she doesn't speak for Max. We all know that." He spat on the floor and glared at Fiona. "And once her daddy dies, I'm gonna turn her into a Hell Kat where she belongs."

"Jim, you couldn't turn a fart into a turd. Sit down." The odds in a fight didn't favor Grier. Jim had always been partial to blades over guns, hand-to-hand battles of strength over finesse fighting. And Grier was still aching from two-punch Hamilton.

"Fuck you, baby traitor."

He pulled the knife.

Shit. That damned thing was more of a sword, both shiny edges gleaming sharp and long enough to gut him in a single stroke.

But Jim was slow and stupid. So if someone was going to challenge Grier, he was glad it hadn't been Nate, Bruce or Frank, or either of the new guys he didn't know.

"I'm going to fuck up what's left of your face, then I'll fight whoever else feels like going. And after I kick your asses, I'm going to take my woman into one of those rooms"—he pointed to the far side of the club where they had stowed some beds for the after-parties that happened almost every night—"and we're going to celebrate our engagement. So let's get this shit done." He turned to Fiona, wrapped a hand around the back of her head and tugged her forward. The kiss, hard and bruising, was as much for show as to put his big fucking mouth to use for something other than inviting the whole club to take a shot at him.

Not that he wouldn't happily rearrange Jim's face, but if he didn't have to, he'd rather remained unbloodied.

Staggered by the sheer pleasure of his tongue swirling inside her mouth, of the taste of her, the little whimper in her throat, and her hands tangled in his hair, he pushed her back. Oh, this woman. Fierce. Potent. Merciless.

The haze over her eyes said she's been equally affected. So, she liked it rough. *Good.*

But right now, Jim didn't seem like a guy inclined to wait for Grier to get laid. He had to be at least forty, probably closer to fifty, but he'd been without his left eye since childhood and had learned to overcome the blind spot by letting his opponent think they had the upper hand. Grier wouldn't make that mistake.

Jim always said he'd been born a Demon and he would die one. And Demons didn't fight fair. "I'm gonna slice your dick off and use it to fuck your old lady."

"Kind of sick, Jim. But at least then you'll be able to

say you have one." Grier hated trash talk but it was Jim's favorite stall tactic.

"Fuck you." He pointed to his chin. "Hit me, baby traitor."

"Traitor I get, but what's the baby about? Is it because you're old?"

The room narrowed as Screaming Demons filed in and Jim's confidence grew to a swagger. He held his arms out to his side and spun in a slow circle. Every man needed to see his mettle.

Grier ignored the cheers and wolf whistles. He focused on the blade in Jim's right then left then right hand. He couldn't remember the last time he'd slept, or ate. But the sliver of light hitting that blade he'd remember for the rest of his life. And the way Jim swung it toward him—a side arc then a quick jerk. Grier saw it coming and moved. The second time, the same move. Then a third. The third lulled Grier into confidence. He could do this all night. But the fourth swing came from over the top and caught Grier's forearm. Fire roared down to his fingertips. Fire and blood.

Son of a bitch.

He jabbed and caught Jim's jaw on his blind side. Stunned and staggering, Jim swung wild, and Grier grabbed his wrist. Which brought Jim's body in close enough he turned his head in a lethal weapon. The crack of his skull against Grier's was the head butt heard around the world. Had to be. Because it rang through every joint, elbow, knee, ankle, and wrist, in Grier's body. His eyes clouded, and birds chirped in his brain.

"Enough."

Not that Grier couldn't have finished it but thank God for Hamilton. The last thing he needed was to embarrass himself by passing out in front of everyone. And the danger was real. He was already bleeding, and he'd probably be cross-eyed for a month.

Jim backed off, holding his forehead with one hand and his jaw with the other. After a couple of breaths, he threw an arm around Grier. "Welcome back, baby traitor."

"Some welcome."

Jim chuckled. "Demon style."

"Yeah." Okay. He hadn't missed everything about the place.

4

Fiona stared at Grier. If he'd been hot two years ago, now he was downright scorching. Even bruised by Hamilton and bloodied by One-eye, there wasn't a Demon in the place or a man in all of New England who compared. Not that she would ever tell him that. And she'd spent years perfecting her game face. It wouldn't betray her. Of course, he'd have to look at her to be able to prove that true. And since that kiss in the clubhouse, he spent all his time not looking at her.

Not tonight, cowboy. She walked out of the bedroom, hair curled, made-up, dressed, and high-heeled. To be honest, though, a thousand-dollar dress didn't feel much different than one of her twenty-dollar dresses.

Grier glanced up from the book he held. "Wow." He cleared his throat. "I mean, you look," he blew out a breath, "wow."

From a man who could make a pair of greasy mechanic's coveralls look like Armani, she'd take the compliment. But she didn't smile and barely breathed because he wasn't wearing greasy coveralls. And he smelled like heaven - rosewood and leather. His button-down was open at the collar, and his island tan made the blond highlights in his honey-colored hair seem even brighter. The gods, Greek or otherwise, had nothing on Grier.

He stood and set the book on the table. "I didn't realize we were getting dressed up."

"Wedding negotiations." She shrugged. "Power suit." At least that was what the saleswoman had called the pencil skirt, high-low ruffled jacket combo. It looked kind of girlie to Fiona but since her fashion sense didn't extend much past tank tops, denim, and leather, she'd handed over her plastic and walked out with the suit.

"We're negotiating?"

"Mostly I'll be deciding, and you'll be nodding." His smile faded, and good God, even his frown made her skin burn. "Don't worry. It's just dinner with Dad."

"Dinner with Max." He sighed. "You could have mentioned your dad was chaperoning our first date."

Date? She'd wanted to date him in high school, wanted to fuck him in college. And now that she was being forced into marriage so she could take over the "family" business, she didn't know what she wanted. A baby. Sure. A nice place. Maybe a picket fence. A dog. Yeah. But Grier? At least he was better than any of the others her dad had proposed.

And of course, choosing Grier would give her the chance for some sweet revenge.

Tonight was about laying the groundwork. She'd be charming, attentive, funny, hell, maybe she'd even throw in some submissiveness, let him be the alpha in their relationship for a few hours. And just when he fell in love, and no doubt he would, she'd kick him straight back to the curb. Literally. With her steel-toe boots.

By then, she'd develop an immunity to his smoky gazes and tingling touches. No matter how many shots of tequila it took.

She picked up her bag. "Ready?"

"Yeah."

Ready to face a firing squad, maybe. A man who wore that deep of a grimace wasn't looking forward to his destination.

Good.

She dangled the keys. "Do you want to drive?" Asking a man like Grier if he wanted to drive a fancy sports car, one of Dad's, was like asking a kid if he wanted ice-cream for supper.

Grier's eyebrows did a zero to sixty toward his hairline. "Grand theft auto?"

"You a cop?" She pulled the fob into her fist. Of all the things she'd considered over the last few days, her father's motives, her own, she hadn't once thought of Grier's. Hadn't considered why he'd left the island with her, without the gun battle or even the argument she'd expected. He'd made it easy even.

And she would have had a better chance of figuring out the mystery if he hadn't moved closer, guided her toward the car with his hand at the small of her back, smelling so good.

The bastard knew it too.

SITTING across from the most beautiful woman in the room, in any room, Grier could barely look away. So far, he'd committed every smile, the flirty, sexy grin, the over-confident smirk, and the she-knew-something-he-didn't beam, to memory, but tonight, she could hide her sadness behind her collection of faux facial expressions. And he ached, deep in his gut to hold her and give her comfort, to help her the way he wished someone had helped him. He admired her bravado though.

She'd dressed like one of those Wall Street warriors (an old girlfriend provided that ditty and he'd never had a chance to use it until now) to sit in her father's house and feed him broth while Grier watched from across the room. These were not the wedding negotiations he'd been promised.

Max spoke quietly when he spoke at all. "I want to talk to Grier." But he stared at Fiona. "Alone."

She shook her head. "Daddy, you should rest." He had good days where he could stand and talk, even come to the clubhouse for a little while before he tired out and went home. Today wasn't one of those.

"For a few minutes, Fi." Max's voice rasped as she grumbled and shot a glare, still sexy as hell, at Grier. But she stood, smoothed her skirt, and left.

The old man's hands shook as he used the electronic controls to sit up further. Then he reached for the rail, and Grier moved to help. "Touch me, boy, and I'll have Ham cut off your hands and feed them to you." Grier held up both hands and backed off. Max coughed once but motioned for him to sit in the chair Fiona had vacated.

Grier waited. Probably for another threat.

"I want your word."

How many times would he have to swear his loyalty? But on the other hand, ten years ago, he'd practically written his oath in blood then left to help Kye keep Eliana safe. So he really couldn't blame Max for his repeated requests for reassurance now.

Max breathed in deep, lungs rattling as he exhaled. "I want your word you'll always protect her and be here for her."

What else could he do, but give Max the promise he wanted, the peace. Grier nodded. "Yeah. Of course."

"This is going to hit her hard."

The right thing to do was to reassure the old man since the doctors had withdrawn all hope. Instead, he nodded. "Yeah."

"She'll need time. And support.'

Grier envied the devotion, the relationship. Not something he'd ever had. God, from the outside, it looked ideal. Of course, he'd been around during Fiona's rebellious stage when her clothes had been black and her eye-makeup as thick as her frown. Back then, everyone thought Max might actually strangle her. But maybe those dark years had strengthened their bond. Of course, all he could do was guess. The closest thing he'd ever had to family was Kye.

He didn't comment even as Max reached for his oxygen mask. "Don't hurt her. Ham will kill you."

Ah. The threat that kept on giving.

"She would have to care about me for me to hurt her."

Maybe she had once, but she'd been young then, so hard to say for sure. She'd flirted, pranced around in clothes no seventeen-year-old or even twenty-year-old woman should have worn in public, and then there was the day at the mall. She'd been twenty. Hadn't cared about the six years' age difference or the fact Max would have him killed. But after he'd walked away, all the previous friendliness disappeared. Right up to the moment he left, she hadn't even looked at him after that day.

"She's angry now. But she has a good heart and you've always had your spot in it." Grier cocked an eyebrow. "Of course, I knew." And yet he'd still thrown them together, made Grier watch her, swear to protect her, maybe even fall for her just a little. And all the while telling Grier to keep his hands off or die. "I wanted her to be happy then. Having you around made her happy. Having you around now will do the same, eventually. She's my baby. I know her better than she knows herself. It's what's keeping you alive." Max motioned Grier closer. "Open the drawer."

Grier looked at the table. Oh, God. What if Max had a gun in there and wanted Grier to end it for him? He swallowed hard. "Max…"

"Just open the damned drawer." He spoke with such force he coughed at the end. "Come on. I'm dying here. I don't have time for you to fuck around."

Grier opened the drawer. Empty except an envelope marked for Fiona. He handed it to Max. "Here."

Max rolled his eyes. "It's for you, dumb ass. Give it to her after I'm gone. The lawyer will take care of the money and the house. But she needs that envelope."

Grier nodded. "Okay."

"And don't let her sissy up my funeral with flowers and church songs. You hear? I want Steppenwolf and bike motors. Got it?"

Not the typical son-in-law speech. "Yeah."

"And get her married now. Don't wait for some big to-do. She needs the comfort of knowing that if I can't be there, she has someone to lean on. Don't you let her fall." Every word Max spoke seemed to wear him down a little more. His breath wheezed, and his chest shook with every inhale and exhale. "I don't have many days left. I want to see my girl married."

Grier nodded. His heart ached for Fiona and the pain she would go through. Not just for her. Max had been the closest thing to a real father figure he'd ever had, too. There'd once been a time when he would have killed for the old man. And it went without saying he would have died for him.

"You will."

Max nodded. "Take her somewhere nice now. Get her the hell out of here."

Of all the things Max had asked of him, getting Fiona to leave would not be the easiest.

* * *

"You want wine?"

He hated the stuff, but Eliana had always insisted they drink it with their dinner. He assumed it was a woman thing. "I'm more of a beer guy."

Fiona breathed a sigh of relief. "Oh, thank God." She chuckled, the strain from leaving her father seeming to dissipate on the ride back to her place. She'd changed from her "power suit" into jeans and a tank before leading him back to a small deck in her backyard.

He lit a fire while she marinated some steaks for grilling. When she handed him his beer, she smiled. "What did Dad say?"

Grier shrugged. Most of their conversation had been for him alone. "That he wants us to get married before he dies. He wants to see you married." He didn't add that Max had told him about the special place Grier held in Fiona's heart. He didn't know what to do with the information yet, so he chose to ignore it.

She took a long pull of his beer. She'd already finished hers. "What did you say?"

He wasn't sure whether he should turn this into a flirty moment with a "hell, yeah" or leave it as it was. "I said okay." He shrugged as if the choice was solely his. "Last wish and all."

Since she was a teenager—Grier hadn't known her

before that—she'd been her father's daughter. She didn't speak without having a good idea of what the other person would say. Not to say she hadn't fumbled through some awkward days, but she'd never put everything out there, except with Grier. He hadn't appreciated that back then.

"How's tomorrow? You free?" She didn't smile. Didn't even look at him now.

"You sure?"

She sighed. "Are you trying to back out? Because Ham—"

Grier had had enough of the Hamilton threat. "I don't give a fuck about Hamilton." He shook his head. "Are you sure you want to do this?" She could choose any of the guys, and the club would follow him because she chose him. Grier was the least likely to stir their devotion. She had to know that.

She stared at him, eyes wide and unblinking. "It's the only way." But her gaze flickered. Her mouth compressed into a line and tears pooled, tipping over her lashes. Oh, God. He couldn't do this. Not if it made her so upset. Of course, she could have been crying over losing her father. It didn't matter. He was going to wrap his arms around her and hold her until she got it all out. Then, they could talk if she wanted to. Or he could go, and they could leave every little detail to rest until later.

He stood and walked around the table, crouched in

front of her and pulled her close. Her tears soaked the shoulder of his shirt, and her sobs tore something inside him. From that moment on, he would protect her. No matter what.

5

Fiona awoke with her head cradled against Grier's chest, his heartbeat a lull to her aching soul. She hadn't handled last night well, had let her emotions go wild, had abandoned her plan and leaned on Grier. Shit.

He opened his eyes and smiled at her when she finally moved away. "Was it good for you?"

Of course, he teased her. Of course, his smile made her heart speed up. And of course, she didn't mind as much as she should. Grier had always had that effect on her, even when he'd walked away from her in the mall. Damned if she understood why. She'd seen nice looking men before. Dated them. Even had sex with a few. But no matter who she kissed or shared her bed with, Grier had always been *the one*.

Still, for appearance sake, she glared. "Must not have been. I slept through it."

His chuckle went straight to her stomach and spread heat. That he'd stayed, let her cry on his shoulder, literally, didn't hurt either. Nothing except her pride anyway.

"So… are we still getting married today?" He still wore his grin but there was a hint of uncertainty lingering in his eyes. Second thoughts probably.

Married to Grier Owen. Mrs. Owen. Years ago, she'd dreamed of being his wife, having his babies, waking up every morning knowing he belonged to her and her to him. Pipe dreams meant for a little girl. Now, everything had changed. The choices had been taken from her. Especially if she wanted to run the club, bring them into this millennium.

Rather than answer his question, she scowled. "Still trying to get out of it?"

He shook his head. "No, ma'am. Excited about the wedding night, is all."

His slow, sultry voice, tinged with suggestion made her blood surge. "Not that kind of marriage." If she'd been trying for conviction in the words, she'd missed the mark, and his smile said he knew it, too. He folded his arms under his head and watched her until she squirmed. "Stop it."

"Stop what? Appreciating my fiancé?" He shook his

head. "Can't do it."

They were lines. She knew what she looked like. Even if she hadn't seen herself every morning of her life, she would know that sleeping in mascara and eyeliner didn't make for a pretty morning Fiona.

"Knock it off, Grier." This time, he stood and came around the bed to stand in front of her. Somehow, through the night—hell, for all she knew she'd done it—his shirt had come open and his six-pack stared at her. "We both know we're being forced into this. We don't have to pretend to enjoy it when we're alone."

He pushed her hair back and tucked it behind her ear. "Maybe I'm not pretending."

And before she could stop her thoughts from shooting out of her big stupid mouth, she asked, "Why now? Why not back then when I wanted you?"

He shrugged, his hand at the back of her head now. "You were too young." He pressured her forward until her only choices were to stand or press her face against his bare stomach. Because the second option would have been awkward, although more desirable than she wanted to admit, she stood. "I was dumb."

When he lowered his head—Jesus Holy Church, when did he get so tall—she turned and his lips brushed her cheek. He smiled. "You're right. Let's save it until the preacher says I'm allowed to kiss my bride." He winked. "It'll build the anticipation." He dropped his hand, and

Fiona missed the touch. Nothing powerful stood in the way of a quick roll between her sheets. Nothing but history and pride. She'd argued with herself about this a hundred times over the last couple of days. Maybe it wouldn't hurt anything. Or maybe it would shred her. She leaned toward it not hurting anything. Leaned hard.

But it would. He'd get the power. He'd know how much she wanted him. And she wouldn't be able to stop her body from telling him what she would cut her own tongue out before she let her mouth say.

She crossed her arms ready to dismiss him. "You need to go. Ham and I'll meet you at the courthouse at eleven."

"Hamilton?"

For the first time, she felt like smiling. "He's my maid of honor. Plus, he's going to be there to make sure you don't chicken out." And that she didn't, but he didn't need to know that.

WHAT DID one wear to marry the guy she'd wanted to marry once but was now being forced to marry? Jeans? Sundress? So much for her big dreams of the long white ball gown. Of the church with flowers on every pew. Of Max walking her down the aisle and handing her over to... Grier. In her fantasy wedding, Grier had always played the groom. No one else seemed to fit in her dream tuxedo.

Oh, God. Grier in a tuxedo. Now there was a thought. Which flowed into her loosening his tie, stripping off his jacket, unbuttoning each button of his shirt with slow, steady hands, lingering at his waistband…

"Did you hear what I said?"

She shook off her lusty imaginings. "What?"

"I said, I'll see you later. At eleven."

She nodded. "Right. Eleven."

And thankfully, before she could make an even bigger fool of herself, Grier left and she fell back onto her mattress.

* * *

Shit. He'd been about two seconds from embarrassing himself on a grand scale, epic even. The kind he wouldn't have been able to flirt his way back from. He drove to the clubhouse in the car Fiona let him borrow. He needed to get ready for the big wedding. His wedding.

He pulled into the lot and dialed Kye's cell. It rang twice while Grier tapped his fingers against the steering wheel.

"Hey, buddy. Glad to see they didn't kill you yet." Kye hadn't thought they would, also he hadn't called since

Grier left, so he obviously hadn't been too worried, either.

"No. Worse." Well, he had to tell someone. Kye was all he had. "Max wants me to marry Fiona."

It took a whole minute for Kye to stop laughing. The bastard. "Marry Fiona. Do you get to be the husband or the wife?"

Grier didn't share Kye's ability to laugh about the whole stinking situation. "Funny."

"You're taking her last name I assume. Mr. Grier Strong. Has a nice ring to it."

"Go ahead, assface. Laugh it up. I'm doing this for your dumb ass."

"For me? Do tell." Kye had no real clue what went down when Fiona came for them, why he hadn't fought leaving with her. She'd made him an offer he couldn't refuse. A lot of that going on in the last few days.

"Never mind. It isn't important."

"So, tell me which one of you is wearing the dress? You know you can't wear white, right?" He let Kye go on for a few more jibes. "Does Max know you're not still a virgin?"

"You about done?"

Kye laughed again. "Hard to tell." He cleared his throat. "You can always come back to the island, you know. We'll figure a way to get you out safe."

He wouldn't even make it to the plane before

Hamilton took him out. And really, did he want to go back? Sure. Belize had been nice. Except for the lonely nights when he'd had too much time to think. Too much time to worry. Too much time to remember. Remember Fiona whether he wanted to admit it or not. What he wanted was what Kye and Eliana had, the friendship, the intimacy, the security of always having someone who wanted them around.

"I think I'm going to see how this plays out." If he needed to go, he would. Eventually.

"Just don't get her knocked up. Their hold on you will kill you if you do." Sage advice from someone who was knee-deep in the thought of making a family.

"How so?"

"Running out on Fiona is one thing. You could do that. But could you run out on your kid?"

Kye knew him better than anyone. Was the only friend he had left in the world.

"No. You're right. No little Grier." No problem since Fiona didn't seem to be interested in anything except getting his signature on their marriage license.

"I'm always right. If you people would just get that through your heads, the world would be a much better place." He laughed. "Hey, Eli's calling me. Let me know how it goes, Mrs. Strong."

Grier signed off with a "fuck you" and hung up. But Kye was right. A baby would tie him to Pine Hill for the rest of his life. And to her, which was the less disturbing of the two propositions.

Good thing Fiona rejected him this morning. Might have stung then, but no way they would've stopped with a single kiss. They would have ended up rolling around her bed probably fighting over who got to be on top. And he didn't have a single condom to his name.

He climbed out of the car and walked past the line of bikes in front of the clubhouse. Damn. He missed riding. Missed the wind in his hair. The speed. The freedom.

He walked in, and Sage, a guy who'd come in just before Grier left with Kye and Eliana, stood. He was about Grier's age with sleeve tattoos and spiky black hair he kept short. "Hey. We need to go collect some past due rents."

"Take somebody else. I have to get ready for my wedding."

"Ham said Max told him it needed to be you."

Of course, he did. He needed Grier to re-establish himself in the business.

Grier nodded. "All right. I need a bike."

"Where's yours?" Sage closed one eye and considered Grier as they walked outside.

"Gone? Parted out I guess?"

Sage laughed. "When did she do that?"

"She who?" God, he missed the quiet of the island,

the not having to deal with people and figure out what the hell they were talking about.

"When you left, we were gonna strip it down, but Fiona wanted it so Max let her keep it."

"Fiona has my bike?" Well, well, well. Wasn't that interesting?

"Hey, man. All I know is she wouldn't let anyone touch it. Max neither." He frowned. "That's how we knew you were actually on club business." He shook his head. "Even Fiona wouldn't have been able to stop Max from destroying it if you'd run out on us."

That lying little minx. "Hey, don't mention that you told me." Not because it would matter. She'd probably only kept it to make him watch her set fire to it if he ever came back anyway. But now that he knew, maybe he could at least have a last look.

6

"Chat the hell do you mean there's a three-day waiting period?" Max might not make it three more days. And if he died before the wedding, Grier could turn tail and run. Even though she'd told him a hundred times what would happen if he did.

The clerk stared at her as if she'd sprouted a second head. "There is a three-day waiting period from the time of application until marriage license issuance. State law. And unless you have a special circumstance, there's nothing I can do."

Grier stood beside her silent, probably thinking this was his lucky day. "Special circumstance?"

"Deployment?"

Fiona wasn't waiting three days. "Hang on." For most of her life, she'd fought her father's influence, hated that he could get anything he wanted with nothing more than a phone call. Now, in this minute, she counted on that influence. Three damned days, her ass.

She took Grier's hand and pulled him out of the clerk's office to the hallway. "What are you doing?"

"We aren't waiting three days. Screw that."

He cocked an eyebrow. "Can't wait to be my bride. I like it."

She frowned, not willing to give him any more fuel with an agreement or argument. "My dad might not have three days left. You said yourself, it's his dying wish to see me married."

And that shut him right up. After a ridiculous rooting around one-handed in her purse for her cell, she let go of Grier to dig with both hands. She found it and dialed. Judge Samuels would help. He'd always liked her dad, and more than once he'd helped the club out of some sticky situations.

She took a minute when he answered to explain the situation. Using her dad as her excuse felt a little too far on the wrong side of morbid, but no other explanation would have convinced him. Plus, she couldn't give Grier any wiggle room to get out of their arrangement.

Finally, Samuels assured her it would be taken care of then he wished her a hearty congratulations, a solemn measure of sympathy for Max, and they hung up. "All right. Got it done."

"And no bloodshed. Nice."

"What makes you think you're worth bloodshed?" Probably, he was. God toyed with her like that.

"Try me." Not quite a dare but close enough. And two could play that way.

She moved in close enough her breasts grazed his chest as she whispered, "You wish," then moved away.

He didn't reply, and his eyes glazed. Oh, yeah. She'd hit her mark. Pure feminine power, like nothing she'd ever felt before rushed through her. Intoxicating. Fresh. Exhilarating.

After a quiet moment, he grinned. "You reading my mind is going to save us a lot of time talking."

"Doesn't take much to read you, Grier. You're trans-parent. Kind of like glass." She smiled, smug, but as nervous as she'd ever been before in her life. In a few minutes or an hour, but by the end of the day, for certain, she would be married to Grier.

She sighed and clasped her shaking hands behind her back.

"Yeah?" He closed his eyes. "What am I thinking right now?"

Oh, good Lord. How the hell was she supposed to know? But she'd let her mouth write a check and now he wanted it cashed. She sighed again. Deeper. Longer. "You're thinking that if I walk away while your eyes are closed, you'll never know."

He widened his eyes and let his mouth hang open for a second. "Holy shit. You really are a psychic."

And he was charming her into a sense of security she didn't have any business feeling. "Stop. Let's get this done and get it over with."

He fanned himself with his hand. "You're such a sweet-talker, Fifi."

She'd taken a few steps away but stopped and turned. "What?"

If ever a man could wipe away his expression and transform himself into a picture of innocence, it was Grier. "I said, you're such a sweet-talker."

He damned well knew what she meant. "Do not, if you value walking upright with a dick between your legs, do not *ever* call me Fifi."

His lips twitched, and he cleared his throat. "But Fif… pet names are important in marriage. Endearments let the other person know you feel intimate toward them. It's healthy." He grinned. "And I'm dying to get intimate with you."

"Keep it up and you're gonna be dying." If he didn't knock off all the teasing, he wasn't going to live long enough to need to find a pet name for her. But threats weren't likely to sway him. She nodded. "Fine. Call me Fifi. And I'll call you…" She tapped her chin with her index finger. "Tiny." She added a suggestive look at his crotch.

He threw his head back and laughed, the sound rich and vibrant, full of legit humor. "Want to check for yourself?"

Yes, she did. And that secret would die with her. "Can we just get through this? Please?"

"Yeah." He sobered, and she missed his smile. There must have been something wrong with her. She went from running cold to nearly melting into a puddle whenever he spoke or smiled or touched her. She didn't want to like him, didn't want to let him have any power over her heart or her emotions. But right now, her frayed nerves needed soothing, and his smile did it.

She held out her hand and tried not to care whether or not he took it. And when he did, her smile came, and she didn't try to hold it back.

"Do you, Kermit Grier Owen, promise Fiona Elizabeth Strong to hope with her, support her, be her favorite person even when she isn't yours, to find adventure with her in every day, to cherish every moment that you share, and love her from this day forward?" The judge, a thirty-something obvious romantic, laid his hand over Grier and Fiona's.

Fiona hadn't looked at him since they'd walked into this room. And before he answered, by God, he would see her face. With his free hand, he curled his index finger and used it to tilt her chin up, so if she didn't want to look at him, she would have to forcibly look away. Finally, she met his gaze, and he smiled. He couldn't help it. "I do."

The judge nodded. "Do you, Fiona Elizabeth Strong, promise Kermit Grier Owen that you will laugh with him, take his side even when he's wrong, be the person he can cry to and with, love him even when he isn't lovable, and to let him know you love him from this day forward?"

She nodded, and the judge leaned a little closer to her. "You actually have to say the words."

Her giggle, nervous, but the sweetest sound he'd ever heard, came with red cheeks and shallow breaths. "I… do."

The judge nodded, and Grier exhaled in a chuckle. Maybe this was more important to him than he thought. Godzilla could have finished the rest of the ceremony and Grier wouldn't have realized. He was too busy memorizing every detail about Fiona and this day. The sparkle in her eyes, the way the sun hit her hair through the window, even the fake bouquet of roses the judge handed to her at the beginning of the ceremony.

"You're married. Now, kiss your bride."

Making the judge tell him twice would have been rude. He slipped his hand into her hair and pulled her forward. No way would she struggle in front of the judge, and if only this once, he would have his way.

His lips brushed against hers, soft at first, but when she wrapped her arms around him and pressed closer, desperation replaced any sense of restraint he might have been able to summon. Not that he tried very hard. He'd kissed her before, more specifically, she'd kissed him, but time had dulled the memory. This was exquisite. Glorious. An out of body experience. One he never wanted to end.

And he would have let it go on and on if the judge hadn't cleared his throat. "Probably better take your celebration somewhere more private."

Fiona giggled just a little then stepped back and touched her fingers to her lips. He had a similar urge. He wanted to savor the feeling of her lips against his, her mouth open, and her tongue swirling with his. The woman kissed with an intensity that robbed him of the ability to breathe, that made his blood flow, no, made it race, south.

He hadn't wanted a woman so badly since… ever. And it took several deep breaths before he could get his shit together. He shook hands with the judge, nodded to Hamilton, then made the mistake of resting his hand at the small of Fiona's back. Just one touch. An innocent touch. And his dick decided it wanted to stand up and say hello like he was some kind of horny teenager who'd just accidentally brushed the boob of the head cheerleader.

She didn't talk. Didn't even look at him. And he was almost positive if it wouldn't have made their entire marriage look like a sham, she would have ridden away with Hamilton. But she let him lead her to the car and open the door for her.

She didn't speak until they were almost back to the clubhouse for the wedding reception. "Kermit?"

He shrugged and started singing the Rainbow Connection. When she didn't smile or join in, he shrugged. "I didn't pick it." Truth be told, he didn't know a damned thing about his name or much about his parents. And that suited him just fine.

7

Fiona walked into the clubhouse ahead of Grier—rather, Kermit—and Hamilton. On any other day, her father in a wheelchair would have made her sad, would have had her bawling like some damned baby, but today, knowing what it took him to load his wheelchair into a car, to appear in front of everyone weak with a catheter bag attached to his chair, made her heart thump its own happy tune.

And she'd put the smile on his face. She'd had to marry Grier to do it, but she'd done it, and if it was the last one she ever saw, at least she'd know she'd helped put it there.

Grier moved next to her, slid an arm around her waist, and leaned in to whisper, "I want my bike back."

She smiled and pulled him further into the room. He could have his bike back. A piece at a time if he wasn't careful. And it wasn't going to be today. Instead of answering, she leaned down to kiss her father's cheek.

He looked up at Grier. "It's done?"

"Yeah. She's all mine now." He made a show of pulling her into his side and kissing the top of her head.

Max nodded, eyelids drooping, hands shaking as he reached to take Grier's hand, which meant he had to stop holding her. Not that she cared. Much.

Okay, she cared a lot. She wanted to hold his hand. Kiss him again. And by all means, have him kiss her again. And again. And again.

She smoothed her hand over her stomach, hoping the butterflies would respond and settle down. When they didn't, she edged closer to her father. In the past, his presence gave her strength and helped her calm, find her inner zen or some such bullshit.

Her heart fluttered when Grier turned his smoky gaze on her. The suggestion, the promise, the heat, all reflected in that look, made her stomach roll. If this was all for show, she'd eat her shoe. Then she'd feed him the other one.

He turned back to Max, and she tuned out whatever they had to say. She studied Grier instead. Imagined him shirtless. She'd seen him once that way a long time ago. And the memory had been the kick-start for her first time with Kenyon Grear, who'd been chosen for his last name alone. She'd never called Kenyon by his first name, preferred pretending, which she could do as long as she kept her eyes closed.

Grier, the husband, and how weird was that to say, had always been built like he worked out just enough to stay lean and trim, but now… with a tan, and the hair… the way his touch ignited every cell in her body… the way his eyes seemed to see through her… at least, if she couldn't have the wedding of her dreams, she could have the wedding night she'd fantasized about since the first time she'd seen Grier. She'd been fourteen. Maybe thirteen.

Grier's arm slid back around her waist and he leaned down to a whisper, "Do you want a drink? Max wants to talk to you, so I'm going to the bar." He nuzzled her ear with his nose.

"Whiskey neat." She'd been avoiding alone time with Max since Grier came home. She didn't want to hear… whatever he had to say. Couldn't bear the thought of a goodbye. "A double."

Grier walked away. Definitely a walk worthy of an extra second of staring. She pulled up a chair and sat so she didn't tower over him in her heels. She wanted to inhale him, to memorize the way he looked, to appreciate the sight of her father as she'd always seen him— powerful, intense, a man to be followed, maybe even worshipped. He was thinner now, more haggard, but still a man who commanded a room.

"Fiona…" He took a long stuttering breath that rattled in his chest. A piece of her heart chipped. "There are things I need to say to you." She waited. Her father wasn't a man who liked his thoughts interrupted by unnecessary noise. "Ham will be watching out for you."

"I have Grier." Kind of.

"And you have Ham if Grier gets out of line or tries to run again. Just in case." He coughed once then shook his head. "He won't be living with you, but he knows he's your protection."

If her dad didn't trust Grier, why did he agree when she threw his name out? Which she'd done sarcastically, thinking he would counter with Nate or Frank. Instead, he'd nodded and started planning to get her *husband* back here. Oh, boy, saying the word was going to take some getting used to.

Instead of asking the question burning in her mind, she nodded.

"Once I'm gone, sell the house. It's paid for. It should bring a nice wad of cash for you. Put half away for the grandkids, keep the other half. Buy a house, set yourself up in a good part of town, good schools, nice playground to push them on the swings. That'll make me happy." This time he grinned. "And your first kid, boy or girl, name it Max. Not Maxine or Maximillian, just Max."

"Of course." That went without saying.

He reached into his pocket and pulled out a piece of paper. "This is your mother's number. She's expecting your call."

"Mom?" Some Hell Kat who'd run off almost before Fiona took her first breath. She'd come back a couple of times. Once for a school play when Fiona was ten. Once when Max spent six months in jail during Fiona's fourteenth birthday. He'd gotten out of jail, and she'd disappeared. Always disappeared.

"For when you need her. And you will."

"I don't need her. *Won't* need her." She needed Max. And this conversation—she couldn't call it a what-if since they knew the ending already—made her stomach churn. Also not a chat she wanted to have on her wedding day.

"Well, you have it just in case."

Fiona's stomach sank. Her father's illness had taken the fight out of him. Before, if she had been this firm, talked back at all, Max would have enforced parental rule, loudly. A slow, deep ached started in her heart and her eyes welled with tears. "Daddy…"

So unfair. She wanted to shake her fist, scream, demand an answer from God. She wanted to crawl onto his father's lap and snuggle into his chest like she'd done when she was a little girl.

He leaned forward and tilted her chin up. "I want to see my girl dance with her husband. I want to watch you cut the cake, and I want you to promise me you'll be happy."

How could she promise that? How could she tell that lie to her father? "I promise." And because she was a woman of her word, because she was nothing without it, she would do whatever it took to make that promise come true.

GRIER WATCHED FIONA. Not because she was doing more than talking to her father, but because the changes in her expression fascinated him. Every emotion played across her features like a little movie that told her story.

When she stood and walked toward him, his gaze dropped to the sway of her hips before he found her smile. It might have looked real to everyone else, but he saw the grim sadness in her eyes even as she crooked her finger at him. He set his beer on the bar and waited. She would come to him, as far as it took. And he would enjoy every second, every seductive glide of her legs, the way, even sad, she was the sexiest woman in the room, in any room, and he would have bet big money on that.

She pressed her body against him, slipped her hands up his chest to twine around his neck. He smiled down at her and clasped his hands at the small of her back. And he would have enjoyed it had Max, the man who'd told him a thousand times to keep his hands off Fiona, not been watching them.

"What are you doing?"

"Giving my dad the show he wants." She brought her hand around to cup his cheek. "He wants us to dance. And cut the cake."

Her voice caught and something unreasonable and possibly abnormal lurched inside him. He just wanted to see her smile. "There's cake?" He grinned. "Best day ever." He kissed her forehead. "Come on, woman. Let's dance so we can get to that. Chocolate or vanilla?" He pulled her into the open space Jez had made by moving tables.

Dancing with Fiona. There were worse ways to spend his afternoon. And this one had been an ups and downs kind of day. Ups - wind in his hair as he sailed down the highway on a bike, watching Fiona's face as he slipped the band on her finger; hell, watching Fiona anytime. Downs - knowing there was no way he was going to be able to go home with Fiona, to hear her moan his name, to feel her skin, slick and hot against his. Oh yeah. And the way his dick got hard just thinking about it.

Someone, probably Jez again, put on a slow song, and Grier drew Fiona in. Oh, God. She fit. Her breasts against his chest. Her breath warming his throat. Her fingers wrapped around his hand. Intoxicating. Sensual.

Soul changing. And this was as far as he would go with her.

"Who told you I have your bike?"

As far as first-dance-as-a-couple conversation went, Fiona needed some guidance. "I'm psychic, remember?"

She shook her head. "You said I was the psychic."

At least, she was playing along. "Tonight, I am."

"What am I thinking then?"

Hell if he knew. All he could say for certain was that when she flipped her hair like that, he could smell her shampoo, and no other fragrance excited him so much. "You're thinking…" He leaned in close, put his lips against her ear and whispered, "You're thinking how much you like dancing with me."

"I was actually thinking I hope I don't step on your toes." She rested her head over his heart and let him guide their swaying bodies. And he knew she *let* him. Had no illusion to any other truth. Nor did he mind. Actually, it made him smile. And he doubted he'd ever be able to wipe that goofy smile from his lips ever again.

He whirled her in a quick circle—showing off for the crowd—and she gasped then giggled. "Like that?" He twirled her out then back in so she thudded against his chest.

"I would've never guessed you had moves."

"Oh, I've got moves." And they weren't singular to the dance floor. Moves he'd be all too happy to show any other woman except Fiona. He just couldn't wrap his head around having sex with her. No matter how badly he wanted her. And, safe to say, he'd never wanted anyone more.

They danced. And ate. Drank more than a few. And nothing wiped the naughty pictures of his wife—wife?—from his mind. Her touches lingered. Her smile brightened. Her words slurred. And finally, it was late enough, they'd done all the traditions, and they could leave. Max had gone early, the crowd had thinned, and they had a driver, so the time to take her home, and drop her off, wasn't going to get any better.

"You ready to go?" She had one arm draped around his waist, and she snuggled under his arm with her other hand hovering just above his belt buckle.

She tilted her head to stare up at him, eyes glazed and dreamy. "Yes, please." Her thumb dipped into his waistband, stroking his shirt just below his stomach.

Oh, God. He glanced at the spot where Max had sat most of the evening. Empty. But he half-expected Max to be sitting there wagging the no-no finger. He shook off his thoughts and nodded to Jez who stuck the first two fingers of each hand into her mouth and whistled.

"Come on, y'all. The bride and groom are ready to start their wedding night. Demon send-off." She waved a finger over her head in a circle then pointed it toward the door.

The bikes had been lined up to make an aisle. Little bags of rice or birdseed had been set on each gas tank. Grier and Fiona stood at the edge of the aisle and waited for the symphony of engines to start, to rev, like a perfectly tuned orchestra before they rushed through, her soft, satin skin wrapped around his more calloused fingers.

Twice during the ride, Fiona dropped her hand into his lap and twice Grier thought about letting it stay, but twice lifted her wrist to move it back to his knee. The first time she'd laughed, the second she huffed out a little breath. She didn't try again. Instead, she leaned her head against the seat and stared out the sunroof of Max's Mercedes until the car pulled in front of her townhouse.

He hadn't really thought this far ahead but climbed out of his side and came around to hers to help her out. She didn't touch him, didn't even take his offered hand. She stomped up the steps leading to her place, her heels an angry clicking sound against the stone walk. When they reached the door, she fumbled with her keys in the lock. "Let me." He opened the door, and she waited on the porch.

"Are you coming in?" Her voice, as wary as it was weary, trembled until he shook his head. Then she found her power. "It's our wedding night."

"In name, Fifi."

"If I didn't want to get laid, I would've married Ham." She cocked her head to the side and smacked it on the brick façade of her house.

Grier pulled her in and kissed the spot she'd injured. "All better."

He would have expected her to pull away since her anger palpitated the air since he'd removed her hand from his crotch. Instead, she slid closer until all of his senses were filled by Fiona. Her perfume, her cheek under his palm—how the hell had that gotten there?—her gaze locked with his while her finger traced his lower lip back and forth. Her soft moan. This moment was all Fiona. Tantalizing. Tempting. Oh, so tempting. Enough he couldn't form an entire thought.

"Come inside."

How many times had Max told him? *Guard her body but touch her and I'll kill you myself.* A potent threat. Of course, back then he hadn't even considered... well, maybe considered, but never acted. His brain couldn't separate the old days from now. And besides a couple of kisses, he didn't need reminding of since they didn't support his argument, this marriage was in name only... for convenience... not real. Although her warm breath at his throat felt real enough.

"I should go." He worked to untangle her arms from where they'd slithered around his neck. Then his waist.

Then she had a handful of his ass. "Fiona!" Wow, that was loud. He lowered his voice, "Fiona."

"We're married, Grier." The hand on his ass slipped around to the front. "And I want you." With his palms, he pressured her shoulders until she stepped back. "You know what? Fine, Grier. If you don't want me, all you had to do was say so."

Oh, God. She had it all wrong. So wrong. The kind of wrong he wouldn't be able to undo until she was sober. "That isn't it."

"You *do* want me?"

"Yes." She started to move in again. "I mean, no. And yes, but not… like this. Fiona…"

"Like what? On our wedding night?"

"As strangers." She growled one of those girl-sounds and flung herself through the front door then slammed it hard enough her front windows rattled. And thank God. Because if she'd persisted much longer, he wouldn't have been able to resist. And nothing good would come from that.

8

Fiona groped around on the table for her bottle of aspirin. Oh, God. It had to be there. She had to find it before her head burst. And the possibility became more real by the second.

She knocked the small white bottle onto the floor then threw herself back against her pillow in a motion so fast her brain couldn't quite catch up and either her bedroom started spinning on its own or her eyes played a serious trick on her.

She threw an arm over her face, shielding herself from the sliver of light leaking in through the slit in her curtain. Maybe today wouldn't be a bad day to explode into a thousand pieces. Especially after she'd somehow, once again, ended up begging Grier to take her to bed. And once again, he'd resisted. Humiliating. On so many levels.

With a groan, she rolled away from the window. Badass biker chick with a husband who wouldn't sleep with her. It would've been a bad TV sitcom plot had it not been her real life. Damn him.

I want my bike back. Well, she wanted him. Guess they both were having a bad week.

She flipped onto her back. "This is stupid." A shower would help. And her bottle of aspirin. Maybe a pair of spiked heels she could grind into Grier's neck. Besides, wallowing in her bed would help no one. Getting up to go in and sort the "rents" the guys collected yesterday would help. The club had business to attend to, and it had been her job since she returned from college to make sure it was taken care of. Maybe it was time for a new era, a new deal, a new way to do things. Yeah. That would make her feel better.

It only took thirty minutes to get ready, another ten to get to the office inside the clubhouse and fifteen more to decide she should have worn shorts instead of jeans. She walked out of the office and looked for Jez. "What the hell? It's like a hundred degrees in here, and it stinks like ass."

Jez stood inside the utility closet handing tools up into the ceiling. "Air isn't working. I'm going up as soon as Cricket takes the damned wrench." She ended on a yell with a tap against the ladder, and a male hand reached from the ceiling.

"Why don't you use the catwalk?" A skinny, metal plank ran the perimeter of the building with cross aisles from one side to the other that made the overhead look like an aerial city map.

"I think the problem is in the duct work. Pretty sure something got in there and died."

"We can call a repair person, Jez."

Jez cocked an eyebrow. "And why would we do that? Cricket and I can do the work. But it's going to take a while for the smell to clear, so why don't you go home and enjoy your husband?"

Fiona rolled her eyes. If only she could, but she didn't even have an idea of where he spent last night. "He isn't here? He, um… got up early and left, I thought to come here." At least she finished strong.

Jez shook her head. "I haven't seen him. Cricket slept here in one of the back rooms. Want me to ask?" Without waiting for an answer, she yelled up into the hole in the ceiling. "Cricket! You seen Grier?"

This kid couldn't have been more than a high schooler, but he already had the hard edges of a Demon. His long, brown hair was tied back with a piece of leather, and he had a scar that ran from the corner of his eye to his jaw and along to his chin. But he had a smile he aimed at Fiona. "Spent the night in the back of the suburban on the lot." He looked Fiona up and down, or rather down and up, since he was hanging upside down.

"If I had a wife like you, you woulda spent the night screaming my name, not sleeping alone."

Jez thumped him in the forehead. "Get back in the hole, fool." When he disappeared, Jez pulled Fiona outside the closet. "You guys okay?"

Oh, God. What could she say to not look like her husband didn't want her? "He… couldn't." The words tumbled out. She hadn't even planned them. But the last thing she wanted to do was admit her husband found her repulsive. This was *way* better. "Then was too embarrassed to stay at home knowing… he let me down."

"Oh, honey." Jez wrapped an arm around her. "He couldn't?"

Fiona shook her head. "Like a wet noodle."

Jez's brow crinkled. "Maybe it was just nerves. You know, being back after so long and jumping into the married end of the pool is kind of a big deal for some guys. Maybe it zapped his mojo."

Zapped? And mojo? Not that would Fiona know. All she'd seen was the back of his head as he turned to get the hell away from her.

And she'd just figured a way to get back at him. "Maybe you could ask around? See how the other guys deal with… faulty equipment? Maybe have Ham or Nate talk to him?"

From above, Cricket chuckled. "I'll do it!"

Jez grabbed a broom from the closet and poked the ceiling. "You'll keep your mouth shut. We clear? Or I will take this broom and make a popsicle out of you." When he didn't answer, she jabbed the ceiling again. "We clear?"

"Yeah. I hear ya." The shout echoed down from the hole.

"Anyway, maybe you could have the guys talk to him? I would appreciate it so much. I don't want him to be embarrassed, and maybe if he knew it happens to all guys…" Her hangover disappeared, and her day brightened by a thousand degrees of light as she pictured half a dozen of the guys sitting around giving Grier counsel about his "problem".

"You bet, honey. Or I could just talk to him."

Fiona shook her head. "Thanks, Jez, but he would die if I sent a woman to talk to him. This is more a guy situation." She could barely keep a straight face.

Jez dropped a hand on her shoulder and nodded. "You're right. Leave it to me. I'll put Ham and Frank on it. And I'm sure One-eye will have plenty of good advice. If any of the guys have experience with limp noodles it has to be Jim."

They shared a quiet chuckle, and Fiona whistled a happy little tune as she flipped her sunglasses down and walked outside.

* * *

Grier stared at Sage. What the fuck had Fiona told everyone? "What?"

"Happens to all of us, Grier." Sage tossed him a little bottle of pills. "Look, no shame in getting a little help with your game. Take one, wait twenty minutes, then…" He shrugged. "By morning, she'll be making you breakfast in bed."

Private matters weren't meant to be discussed out here, around a roaring fire in the clubhouse parking lot. And no mistaking, his dick was a private matter. But Frank came around behind him. "Happened to me last week. Had that new Hell Kat, Bridget, on her knees, ready, and all of a sudden, my sword isn't made of steel anymore."

Sword?

Frank continued undaunted by the chortles of laughter. "Yeah, well, next night I ruined her for all you morons."

Grier didn't need to hear this shit. He needed to grab Fiona, throw her onto the bed and show her his equipment had been at permanent attention since the very moment she turned up on the island to bring him home. And then she'd damned well know *that* wasn't the problem.

Hell, he hadn't seen her in a week almost, and just

the thought of her had the tip of his dick wet and threatening a peep show out the waistband of his jeans.

Thank God for the ringing phone so he didn't have to try to come up with some excuse for whatever tale Fiona had decided to tell. "Hello?"

She sniffed, and he heard the tears before she ever spoke. "Can you come to me?"

He would have thought it a trick had she not sounded so sad, so devastated. "Is it Max?"

"Yes. The nurse… called." Her voice broke, and a sob rang down the line to settle in his heart. "Please, Grier."

He was already on his borrowed bike, helmet on. "I'm on my way." He slid the phone into his jacket and rode like the wind to her place. She was outside and climbed on behind him almost before he rolled to a stop. Not the right time to think about her arms around him or her perfume on the air, the way she held on as if she could drain his power with her touch, but he did focus on those things. When he should have been comforting her, helping her through the next and most difficult part of her life, all he could think of was crushing her mouth with his, drinking her in, and touching her in places he'd dreamed of every night since the wedding.

Driving kept him sane, kept his hands busy and his eyes on the road. He stopped at the light on Sprig and laid his hand over hers where they clasped around his waist as he checked for traffic. He'd run a thousand lights in his life, never cared before, but he'd never had Fiona on his bike when he did. He waited for a truck then zoomed through.

A few more blocks and he turned into her father's drive. She kept the helmet on as she climbed off the bike and ran up the stairs to burst through the door. He found her standing by her father's bed, face stoic, eyes dry as she held his hand. Max didn't move, hardly breathed, probably had no idea his daughter had arrived.

Grier steadied her with a hand on each of her shoulders as she watched her father. Not that she needed steadying. She didn't sway or even let him know she knew he was there. Unless leaning her head back against his chest counted, but he couldn't be sure she meant to. Still, he didn't step back. Instead, he worked to fight enjoying the feel of her against him.

Max's chest rumbled then rattled on a last shaky breath, and he drifted away, not in the blaze of glory he'd always said he dreamed of, but quietly. No hail of gunfire or accident on his bike. Just as an old man in his bed, with his daughter at his side and a nurse monitoring his heartbeat. The machines went silent, not at all like he'd seen on TV when a heart flatlined, but in a stillness as loud as any sound he'd ever heard.

Fiona brought his knuckles to her lips, kissed them then laid his hand across his stomach, hers lingering as if she could capture the essence of him with her touch. "Bye, Daddy."

Her knees bent, and Grier held her up until she turned into him. She didn't sob, or scream, or even breathe hard. Gentle tears rolled down her cheek and soaked the front of his shirt as she clung to him.

He ran his hand over her back in small circles, hoping it was comfort enough because he damned sure didn't know a single word to say. He would deal with his own grief later, with mourning the man who'd taken him in and showed him how a real man walked and talked, how he should treat a woman he loved and how he should put family, although Max had meant the club, above all else.

The nurse made the calls to the funeral home where Max's body would be prepared and to report the death, but Grier would have to call the club. Not until Fiona had herself under control, though. Until then, he would hold her, comfort her in the only way he knew how.

"We should go," she finally whispered.

"Do you want to take one of the cars?"

She shook her head. "No. The bike." With her eyes closed, she added, "Please."

Almost every day, he would deny her nothing in his power except the one thing she seemed to want most. Today, he would deny her nothing.

9

Fiona didn't want to need him. Or want him. She did. But need him… one night only. She would lean on him tonight and never again. She rested her cheek against his back as he breezed them down the side roads between her father's house and her own.

She had a pain, one so stark, so shrill, she didn't have the defenses to fight it. Since she was a little girl, Max had been her world. She talked to him every day whether they were angry at one another or not. He'd seen her through broken hearts, a missing mother, when her best friend, Sherry Cahill, decided to be best friends with Melanie Keen instead of Fiona, through her first time shaving her legs, driving lessons, graduations… and he'd only been gone an hour and already she missed him with an ache so powerful, she lost her grip. One hand fell away and Grier pulled it around him.

Awareness of every cell in her body, because she could feel pain in all of them, rang through her. He'd told her once she'd know a pain that would make her want to die. It was after a fight they'd had because a boy, Grier, though she hadn't told her father, had broken her heart. He'd tried to empathize, told her how he felt when her mother ran away, but she'd been so devastated, so diminished. The only way she felt whole was to fight. To let her anger light her way. But Max had…

She sobbed. Her nose ran. Her eyes swelled. And still, damned if she could stop. Max had never been just a dad or a father. He'd been a daddy. All her life. Even when she'd called him anything else.

And now he was gone.

Grier pulled the bike in front of her house and shut down the engine. She should let go, get off the bike, and go inside, but tonight, she didn't want to be alone. As if he knew, he covered her clasped hands with his and waited. Quiet. Still. Until she was ready to ease away, to stand on her own.

Asking him to stay made her weak, or maybe he made her weak, but it didn't matter. The thought of going into that house alone, the idea of missing her father without someone to comfort her made her want to drink. And the last thing anyone needed was drunk, sad Fiona on the loose.

"Will you stay?"

"Yeah." He hung her helmet on his handlebar and walked beside her up the steps. She opened the door and flipped on the light then led him inside. Her legs, her arms, her head, no part of her had the strength to hold her weight. She collapsed on the sofa and before the second wave of sadness hit, Grier gathered her against him, wrapped her in his arms, and kissed the top of her head.

"I'm so sorry, Fi."

She nodded and sniffed back the tears. "He liked you."

"He liked you, too." She looked up at his sympathetic smile, and he squeezed her a little tighter.

"You know what I mean. He didn't want to believe you would run away like that." She rested her head over his heart, let the steady beat lull her. She concentrated on it until the ache behind her eyes quieted.

Grier nodded and laid his cheek on the top of her head. "I remember when I first met him. I was sixteen. Street kid. Stupid. Max came up, said some football jock was harassing his kid. He said if I handled it, he'd help me. Get me in the club."

She sat back. One day Robby Fitch had been an ugly

thorn poking her, teasing her for her braces and braids. The next day, Max had paid for a makeover, and Fitch came to school with a broken nose, two black eyes, and a couple of broken fingers. But he'd never teased her again, and he made sure no one else did either. "That was you?"

"Yeah."

Max. Max. Max. "And Cooper? Ryan Fielding?" She groaned. "Cameron?" Now there was a boy who'd had potential.

"Max just wanted you to find someone who was good enough for you."

Despite her better judgment, she snuggled closer. "And I guess he thought that was you."

"I guess. You could have ended up married to that loser Cooper O'Shea. Drop-out. Spends his time looking at online porn after he leaves his job folding clothes at the Old Navy."

Fiona managed to pull away enough to look at him. "How do you know?"

"Sage. Max gave him my job after I… left. But Sage is a computer savant. He knows stuff."

Stuff? For a moment, she forgot her father had passed away, forgot the ache in her heart. But now, the pain rocked through her, stole her breath. She closed her eyes again and listened to his heart. Grier kissed her head again and tightened his hold. She nestled in, absorbing his warmth.

"I need a drink." She pulled away, and he let go and stood.

"Stay here. I'll get it." At the doorway between the kitchen and living room, he turned to gaze at her. "Fiona…"

She couldn't hear more sentiment right now. It would destroy her, break the very thin wall holding her together. "Vodka in the freezer. Tumblers in the cabinet." He didn't move until she said, "Please."

With a nod, he retrieved the alcohol and a couple of glasses then came back to sit beside her. He didn't speak, just poured her drink, and handed it to her, then moved to sit against the cushions and pull her into his arms again.

She shook her head and struggled out of his hold. "You won't even drink with me on the worst night of my life?"

He reached for her again. "Another night I'll toast Max with you. Tonight, I'm taking care of you." He kissed the top of her head again. "My wife."

Wife? Now he wanted to claim marriage? Then, as if she really could see inside his head, she smiled. "I'm not going to fight with you, Grier."

"Who said I want to fight?"

She held her glass in one hand and his cheek in the other. "You don't. But if it's what I want or what I… need, you'll fight back." And it would make her feel better for a minute. The way the reminiscing had. She leaned in and brushed her lips over his, softly, lingering until her eyelids fluttered shut, and he yanked her across his lap.

This. For God's sake, this.

OH, God. This woman. She'd kissed him when they were younger—would that mall scene in his head never go away?—but this was more intense, desperate, but closed. Her heart wasn't in it. And while he would have been fine with that had she not been grieving, the simple fact she'd lost her father today made this a no-go. No matter how many times she whimpered into his mouth, or how her hands twisted his shirt out of her way so she could knead the skin at his spine, he couldn't let her do this.

And his resolve held firm until she guided his hand to her thigh. Her smooth, firm, supple thigh. Skin like satin. Warm. Inching apart because her skirt held tight. The hand guiding him stopped, and she used it to jerk the fabric toward her hips.

If he didn't stop soon, he wouldn't be able. They would end up rolling around her floor and her couch and probably her kitchen table and it would be an amazing, exquisite experience. But in the morning, she would regret it. He would regret it. If he'd not been so stubborn, not so caught up in his memories of Max's threats, they would already have had a first time, and a second and so many more, and this sex would be therapeutic, not a first time shadowed by Max's death.

She moaned into his mouth when he slid his hand a sliver closer to her panties, to the heaven they guarded. Barely guarded. She twisted, and his hand shifted closer, brushed her silk-covered clit, and she moaned again. Primal. Raw. She writhed and strained, but this time he held her in place.

He tore his lips away and moved them along her jaw until he could take her earlobe between his teeth. "Tell me what you want, Fiona."

She tried to draw his hand inside her panties, but he didn't budge.

"Tell me, Fiona." By now, he could have used his cock to cut diamonds, and he wanted the sweet bliss of release, but Fiona needed the mindlessness and collapse an orgasm, the one he planned to give her, would bring.

"I want your fingers."

She tried to capture his face between her hands, and he twisted away. He traced her lips with his thumb. "What do you want me to do with them?"

She opened her mouth and dragged her teeth along

the pad of his thumb, then circled his wrist and brought it to her thigh, tried to push his hand again. Again, he didn't move.

"If you want me to finger you, ask me to do it."

"Grier, please." Desire thickened her voice, and Grier's heart threatened to pound out of his body through his dick.

"Please, what?"

She narrowed her eyes, and he won their power play. With her teeth clenched, she hissed the words. "Please fuck my pussy with your fingers."

Slow. Deliberate. He slithered the backs of his fingers up her thigh. She gasped when he skipped around to the waistband of her panties and hauled them down to her knees as he crushed her mouth with his.

Oh, God. So much more exquisite than he'd ever imagined. Wet and hot. Grier imagined his cock sliding in and out, closed his eyes and tried to remember tonight was for Fiona. He swiped his thumb over her clit, and she gasped again.

Her moan, low and deep, long and pleased, came when he slid his finger inside, still teasing her with his thumb. "Unbutton your blouse."

She needed someone to take control, to let her enjoy without thinking.

"What?"

"Fiona, unbutton your blouse." He spoke in a firm, determined tone.

She was already panting in time with every gentle thrust of his fingers. It wouldn't be long. "I can't."

"I could do it, but then I have to stop this." He slipped his fingers out, and she brought hers to fumble with the buttons on her shirt. "Good." When she finished, she pulled it open, exposing see-through lace, the kind of bra meant to entice, to tempt, to make a man lose his damned mind. And what those transparent cups held underneath… he was maybe ten seconds from making an embarrassing high school mistake.

He needed to slow this down. Take a minute to get his shit together. He removed his fingers. "Stand up. Take your clothes off." Without the argument he might have expected, she stood and shimmied out of her skirt, slipped out of her shirt, shucked the bra and panties before he could even blink.

Naked Fiona did nothing to help his control. Quite the opposite, in fact. She was everything he'd dreamed her to be and more. So much more. Curves and plains, edges and angles. He took a few seconds to drink her in, to feast on her body with his eyes.

He scooted to the edge of the sofa and pulled her in so that her belly button was at his eye level. "Tell me what you want, Fiona." Because he damned sure knew what he wanted.

"Fuck me, Grier."

Oh, God, yes.

Focus.

"Later. Pick something else."

"Take your clothes off."

"No. Try again." He brought one of her hands to his mouth and sucked her fingers, laving them with his tongue. When he withdrew them from his mouth, he used them to tease her nipple then blew softly until it pebbled. This time, he licked her fingers and watched her watching him. Her eyes clouded, and she threw her head back. By far the most erotic thing he'd ever seen.

"Lick me, Grier."

And he couldn't wait any longer, couldn't make her ask for more. He flicked his tongue over her clit, once, twice, again, always withdrawing until she tangled her fingers in his hair, holding him against her.

He pulled away long enough to spin her to her back on the sofa. "Tease your nipples for me, Fiona." She had her eyes closed but moved her hands to her breasts. He bit his lip to keep from groaning even as his cock twitched, straining against his jeans. He situated between her legs, licking, teasing, fucking her with his fingers while she kneaded her breasts and tweaked her nipples. This was hotter for him than any sex he'd ever had. And that was before she bucked and twisted, screamed, and whimpered. Before she cried out his name and pressed her heels into the sofa cushion to bring her hips higher.

Tonight might have started out for Fiona, but it ended with her in his arms, covered in a blanket she kept on the back of the sofa. A night he would remember for as long as he lived.

10

Five days so far. Fiona had survived five days without her father. She shivered and reached to the panel in front of her seat to switch down the air conditioner. Even inside the limousine with the tinted windows up, she could hear the roar of motorcycles. Hundreds of them. The Demons leading the hearse and limousine, other clubs falling in behind, the death of a well-respected leader blurring the lines between hate and admiration, between discourse and saying goodbye.

Grier sat beside her, not touching. He hadn't even looked at her since that morning—was it only a week ago?—when she awoke, naked with her body wrapped around his. He'd not even stayed long enough for her to get out of the shower. Oh, he'd done the husband things required when a father-in-law dies. He'd helped her order flowers, pick a casket, arrange the service, but beyond holding her hand as she sat in the funeral director's office, she hadn't so much as laid eyes on him until now.

She glanced over now. Even in profile, he was beautiful. The kind that made her mouth dry and her heart thump, even on the day she had to look at a box to say goodbye to her father. He stared out of the window, probably wishing he was on a bike, leading her father to his final resting place. But he slid his hand across the seat and threaded their fingers together, gave her a squeeze that offered comfort, to remind her she wasn't alone. At least, she interpreted it as such.

The car turned, drove down a long, paved lane to pull in front of a short stone mausoleum with pillars and angel statues. Had she chosen the right place? Putting her father's ashes in a crypt instead of keeping them with her?

Tears slipped down her cheeks, and she swiped them away with the palms of her hands. The driver came around to open her door. No rider would dismount until she stepped out and went to the hearse to carry the urn to the place where it would remain.

Maybe if she thought of it that way, separated the idea of her father from the black glass urn emblazoned with a motorcycle on its face, she could get through this with her heart intact. She took a deep breath and pictured Max, stern, but gentle. *You can do this,* he would've said. *Get out of the car and put me away where I belong.*

And she would have been fine had Grier not turned her chin to face him. "I'm here, okay?"

She should have been seething with anger. Should have resented him for leaving her to wither through the nights alone, to suffer her thoughts with no one to talk to, no one to be with her as she agonized her losses and the choices she'd made. Instead, she nodded. Let his touch soothe her.

"Thank you."

Her chest ached, the tangible pain of a broken heart, but she owed Max so much. The least she could do, the very least, was honor him in a way that would make him proud of her, that would show her strength, her respect, how much she loved him.

She climbed out of the car, and only then did Grier step out on his side and come around to stand beside her. He guided her to the hearse where she stood, surrounded now by the Demon brotherhood her father had created. Frank and Nate, two of her father's most trusted friends, flanked her and Grier while the others fell in. Jez had ridden with Nate, and she stood a step behind Fiona, tissue-dabbing her eyes with one hand and squeezing Fiona's shoulder with the other. Jez had been her father's "special" friend.

One-eye Jim stood to the side of the hearse, his head

bowed and his eyes wet. All these men, the strongest she'd ever known or met, stood there with tears and shaking shoulders. Her men now.

The thought humbled her, and she glanced into each of their faces. She would earn their respect. She would lead them. She would make sure her father's legacy live on, survive for generations into the future.

Grier nudged her shoulder as Jim handed the urn to Frank who handed it to Jez who handed it to Nate who handed it to Nicky. On her father's ashes went so each man could have a second holding greatness before it made its way to Grier who handed it to Fiona.

Fiona closed her eyes, held the urn then followed the preacher into the crypt. Her father would have hated this whole thing. He would have wanted to go out in some hail of gunfire, with a lot of alcohol, a lot of women, and all the guys sitting around talking about their glory days, more specifically the way back whens of her father's glory days, when no other group dared question the Demons. Instead, she'd hauled him out here, to a cemetery in the middle of nowhere, where he would be alone... all alone for eternity.

She'd only walked three steps, but turning back, it looked like miles. She searched for Grier in the crowd, and when she found him, she shook her head. "I can't do this."

He broke through the crowd of men watching her

and closed the distance between them. She held her father with an arm crooked around the urn and held Grier with the other around his waist. The symmetry made her smile. Always between them. Where Max had been in life and where he would be in death.

Hands shoved in his pockets, Grier cocked his head, waiting.

"My dad doesn't belong here." She gestured to the building behind her. "He belongs with us. With them." As she glanced away from Grier to the men, the ones who would celebrate her father long into tonight, she knew this was the right thing, the thing her father would have wanted.

Grier nodded and turned to the funeral director who stood beside the hearse. Fiona didn't hear what they discussed, but when Grier came back, he took her hand. "Let's take him home."

This was the right decision. One she could be proud of. And her first as the head of the family business.

* * *

"Could you say that again?"

No way could Grier have heard what he thought he'd heard. He needed to hear the words again. Maybe then his mouth would shut, and he could go on with his life. Single again. Because no damned way had Max added a clause like the one the bad-toupee wearing lawyer had just read.

Instead of reading from the blue-backed pages in his hand, the lawyer set them down and removed his wire-rimmed glasses. "It means Fiona can run the companies attached to the Screaming Demons motorcycle club for the term of two years provided the two of you are married. Should your marital status change or the circumstances of your living arrangements—" He cocked his chin to one side and stared at Fiona who hadn't moved since he'd finished reading. "You do live together?"

"Currently? No." Her voice wavered as she glanced at Grier.

"Well, you must occupy the same home for the term of two years or the business will be sold immediately and the Screaming Demon Motorcycle club will be dissolved, and all the proceeds from the sale of Max's house, the businesses, and the other properties Max holds in the name of the motorcycle club will go to the members of the club, excluding the two of you. You will each receive a one-time thousand-dollar pay-out."

Grier checked Fiona from the corner of his eye. She sat stoic, quiet, unmoving. Part of him wondered if she'd known this all along. The other part couldn't process the information. Couldn't understand what this all meant, why Max would want to bind Fiona to him, even if only for two years.

And the lawyer continued. "The grandchildren clause is very specific."

"Grandchildren clause?"

Oh, Max. What did you do?

"Yes. It states that Fiona, barring medical issues, has one year to get pregnant. Half of the inheritance will be held in trust for the grandchildren." He picked up his glasses and held them in front of his face rather than slipping them on. "Should Fiona not become pregnant within the first year, the trust will be dissolved and the money held by Kessler and Feinstein, Attorneys at Law."

"Your firm?"

"Yes. Your father—" He stared at Fiona now and let his eyes wander over her body so that Grier clenched his fist to keep from killing the old fucker. "—was very specific."

This tied Grier to Fiona, and the quickie divorce they'd discussed only yesterday was no more. He could see it in her face, in the hope written in her eyes. She *wanted* a baby, *wanted* to make him a father. The man least likely to be good at it.

And if he worked like a dog for the rest of his life, there was no way he could make enough money to buy her out of this. No way he could match the inheritance or even come close enough to convince her to set him free of this ridiculous bargain he'd struck.

Fiona stood, walked to a table set with a decanter of dark amber whiskey and matching crystal glasses. She poured four fingers into a glass and drank in one long gulp. Then she poured another. "Fi, what are you doing?"

"I am horribly sober and looking to change that. I'd put out the do-not-disturb sign, but—" She snapped her fingers. "—apparently, I have to be disturbed." She widened her eyes and stage whispered, "sexually."

"Miss Strong—"

She held up her glass in a toast. "It's Mrs. Owen, now, Mr. Kessler. Or did Harvard Law not teach reading comprehension?"

"Mrs. Owen, the terms are quite clear and specific, but he also left you both an escape. You lose everything, including the inheritance for the children, but..." He shrugged. "It's a way out."

"Which is?" Well, someone had to ask. Might as well have been Grier.

"If Fiona is in danger or abused, she may leave the relationship unscathed."

"And what happens to Grier?"

Kessler hung his head. "There's a number that needs to be called by Fiona." He handed her an envelope. "What happens to Mr. Owen after the call is not mentioned. But considering the nature of the secrecy and your father's business interests…"

Nothing much to guess there. Grier closed his eyes and tilted his head back. He needed to think, to process, to make a new plan. When he opened his eyes, Fiona held out a drink. The lawyer stood and walked to the door. "I'll give you a minute."

Fiona sank into the chair next to him. She chuckled once. Then again. By the time he turned to her, she'd dissolved into almost hysterical laughter.

"Fi…"

Either she couldn't stop or wouldn't. She calmed enough to speak, but it took a while. "That old bastard."

Any other time and under any other circumstances, he would have laughed with her. Would have enjoyed a good chuckle. But now, watching his life circle the drain, along with Fiona's and a child to be named later, he couldn't find so much as a smile.

11

Fiona looked from the man in front of her to the glass of whiskey in her hand. "Drink, Mr. Sedotal?" He shook his head. "All right then. You understand you won't be a member of the club. I don't want you looking like one of them or talking like one of them. If I hire you, you're my man in black, my protector."

Tyler Sedotal. Ex-Marine. Three tours in Afghanistan. Home long enough to get arrested, sentenced, serve his time, and be released. She'd found him waiting for a ride outside the prison. But the lure of an Italian sports car and the banded stack of bills persuaded him into her car.

"Why do you need protection?"

She smiled because she had pieces to move around the board. Tyler Sedotal was her pawn. "I don't."

"My price—"

She slammed her glass down. "Mr. Sedotal, look around you." Her father's Spanish oak desk had been traded for a glass and steel one that sat in the lower quarter of the office with a new white leather chair behind it. The paintings had been upgraded, the floor polished to a glossy, white shine she could see her reflection in. "Your price isn't an issue."

"As your protection, I will be in control. I will screen your guests, your clientele, and I alone carry inside this building. Or no deal."

She narrowed her eyes. After a moment, she slid open a steel-fronted drawer and slid a pistol, a semi-auto Glock, the one thing of Max's she'd kept in the office, onto the desk. "Can I call you Tyler?" He nodded, his somewhat bored expression turned on her. The gun sat between them, hopefully a reminder of exactly who was in charge of this meeting. "Tyler, obviously you know this isn't just any normal business. We deal with some… unsavory product which means we deal with some unsavory buyers and sellers. My guys carry out of necessity, because they're sworn to protect one another and this club at all costs. I wouldn't, and you won't, ask them to put their weapons down and still risk their lives." She stood and held out her hand, not touching the gun because to show fear was to show weakness. And Fiona Strong-

Owen was anything but weak. Not after the month she'd had.

"Can I call you Fiona?" She shrugged and crossed her arms since Tyler didn't seem in any hurry to end their meeting. And it didn't matter what he called her so long as he took the job. She had interests to protect. Hers. And the child she would have one way or another. She needed discretion. But more, she needed eyes on the street, someone whose loyalty didn't belong first to her father and the club which only transferred to her by default. This guy came recommended, and his allegiance would be to her. Because she was more than willing to pay for it.

She watched him, stared hard. He was blond, not like Grier's honey-blond, but lighter. And he had green eyes. He was older than Grier, not as built, but she would have bet big money he didn't need strength to be fast enough to stymie an opponent. Fast enough to challenge Grier should the need arise.

She glanced over her shoulder at Hamilton. She wanted to see how Tyler Sedotal took a punch. Without speaking, she tapped her fingers twice on the blotter on her desk. Hamilton remained still. He would wait until the last moment then he would pounce.

"I can't have you telling me how to do my job. For our relationship to work, for me to be the man in your life who protects you from whatever dangers come to your door, I have to have your total trust and your complete cooperation. When I say no one carries a weapon except me, it's for your safety." She cocked her head. "Obviously, with your father's death, you have questions now about your men trying to overthrow you. Your husband, maybe?"

Word had obviously made it to the street that some of the Demons were less than thrilled with pulling out of the drug game. For years, it had meant big pocket money and not just a couple had been pissy about losing that kind of income. She'd let the ones who wanted to leave go, Bruce, two new guys and Dan, and she'd known there would be blow-back on the streets, but not to the level it had escalated to.

She didn't answer, and Sedotal continued. "And your husband will need to be briefed on our contact." He spoke with military precision, a command that meant he'd been in charge somewhere.

"Our contact?"

"I can't protect you if I'm not with you. Since your husband has taken to sleeping at the club"—and how the fuck did he know that?—"I'll be staying at your place."

No, the hell he wouldn't. She sat back, needed to think for a minute. Anyone she hired for "security" would likely make the same demands. Particularly if Grier wasn't staying there. Well, she would fix that, and

Sedotal could stay at the clubhouse since that was where she needed him anyway.

* * *

GRIER PARKED THE BIKE, dangled the helmet over the brake handle. And he watched. Watched Fiona stalk her way across the lot to him. To stand in front of the bike, hands on hips. As pretty in all black as when she'd worn the yellow sundress in high school and the blue power suit a few weeks earlier.

"Hello, beautiful."

She crossed her arms, feet apart, eyes narrow. No other warrior ever looked so hot. "You're staying at home tonight. And every night from here on out. Clear?"

Sage cleared his throat and hid his smirk behind his fist. Grier punched him in the chest. "Beat it."

He waited until Sage walked into the clubhouse before he turned to her. "Fiona."

"Grier, I'm your wife. And every damned person here knows you don't want me and you don't want to be married to me." She ran her hand through her hair, flipped it to one side, and sighed. "Could you just pretend for a while that we're together? Maybe save me some embarrassment?"

"Pretend?" His brow crinkled. Pretend? Well, yeah,

but not the way she thought. Not a way he could live with himself if she believed. He swung his leg over the bike, stood and strode to her, tangled his hand in her hair and kissed her. Hard. Desperate. With enough passion, she certainly wouldn't be able to accuse him of pretending ever again.

When he'd proved his point and before he lost consciousness, he let her go. To his credit, he didn't sway or stagger or fall to smack his probably goofy-grinning face on the concrete. He stood staring.

"Nice performance. I'd ask for an encore, but we both know…"

Before she could finish, he kissed her again. As much because he didn't want to hear the rest because he needed to pull her body in, to taste her mouth, feel her skin. His world went dark with Fiona as the only point of light. Every breath came because of her, at her command. And damned if he cared. He wanted her.

"Get on the bike, Fiona."

"I need to talk to you."

He handed her the helmet. "There isn't going to be any talking, Fiona. There will be moaning. A lot of moaning." He wanted her in the dark, dangerous way that crowded reason out of his head. "Now get on the bike, or I'll put you on it."

Their staring contest lasted only as long as it took her to pop the helmet over her hair and adjust the strap. If she wanted proof he wanted her, tonight and tonight only, he'd give her all the proof she could handle.

GRIER WANTED FIONA. Plain and simple. But nothing about their relationship was easy. There was too much outside interference from a dead man. It clouded everything, made Grier nothing more than Fiona's cash cow. But for now, as he drove to her place with her hand rubbing his cock through his jeans, he didn't give a damn about Max or two-year marriages and the introduction of a baby into this mess. All he cared about was Fiona.

At the stoplight, he twisted to kiss her, just a taste of what was to come. A tongue-swirling tease. Oh, God, this woman. When the light turned, he raced toward her house, her hand still stroking, his dick still standing at attention.

It wasn't until he pulled into her driveway around one of Max's cars that he made his plan. Tonight, he would give Fiona what she wanted, what they both wanted, then he would get up and leave. And he would make her understand they couldn't bring a baby into their fake relationship. He would be the guy she expected him to be, an asshole who only looked out for himself and didn't stick around for the after-glow cuddle.

He helped her off the bike, pulled her up the steps and waited while she worked to unlock the door. She didn't have them completely inside when he turned her and backed her against the wall.

The kiss was meant to mark her, to make her as desperate as he felt. Years of pent up passion pulsated inside him, begging for release. He held her hands over her head as he ran his tongue down her throat to her collarbone while his free hand cupped her breast and his hips ground against hers.

So perfect. Desire rocked him, made him want to lay her down on the floor and take her. *Stick to the plan.* He broke away. Took two full steps back, panting as if he'd just run the four-minute mile.

He wanted her so badly he couldn't see anything but her swollen lips, her heaving breasts, her heavy-lidded eyes. It took all his will, every ounce of self-control he possessed not to go to her and continue. "Go put on something sexy." Not that he needed her to change clothes to turn him on or that what she was wearing wasn't sexy enough. He just needed the time to pull himself together.

"I could just take this off." She shucked her shirt, tossing it onto the back of the sofa. Her nipples strained against another of those barely-there lace bras and any blood that might have been left in his brain went straight to his dick.

He didn't answer just stared at her. Because he couldn't speak, couldn't form words with his tongue lolling half down his throat.

She licked her lips and squeaked out an "okay" before she turned to go up to her room. Grier went to the kitchen, didn't bother with a glass, pulled the vodka from the freezer, and took a long, necessary drink. Then another before he returned to the living room and gave the staircase a thoughtful glance. Heaven waited at the top of those steps. Probably a little hell, too.

Before he made it halfway, some asshat knocked at the front door, an asshat with really bad timing.

Grier considered ignoring it but turned and went back. As he swung the door open, a man, tall, blond, tattooed, and dressed all in black, stood on the porch. And since Grier wasn't in the mood for pleasantries, he didn't bother. "What do you want?"

The man pushed past him. "Fiona around? She hired me today as security, and I'm here to clear her place."

"Her place doesn't need clearing." Something about this guy, the predatory look around, the way he walked to make himself seem taller, the way he plopped on the sofa to wait for a Fiona who was otherwise engaged, pissed Grier off. "Get out."

The guy shook his head. "Can't do it. Need to make

sure the lady is okay with you as her protection." The cocked eyebrow and the up and down look was overkill insulting.

Grier chuckled without the mirth. "You have a name? I like to know whose ass I'm kicking when I'm kicking it."

And he had the nerve to laugh. "Tyler Sedotal. Fiona's personal security."

"I'm Fiona's personal security."

"Apparently, she doesn't think so." He kicked his boots onto her coffee table and laced his fingers behind his head. "Maybe she thinks you're planning on running off again." He shrugged and Grier's blood boiled. "If I was you, though, I wouldn't worry about what your woman thinks. I would worry about what your men think that your woman went behind your back and *hired* someone to protect her." He widened his eyes. "Oh wait. They're *her* men, aren't they?" He pursed his lips. "So, tell me, what does that make you?"

"That makes me the guy who's going to kick your ass out of here." He moved, grabbed the prick by his shirt and yanked him to his feet.

In Grier's defense, Tyler took the first swing. It thrust Grier backward, into the hanging television that crashed to the floor. Grier rebounded and caught Tyler's jaw with a right hook. He staggered but stayed on his feet and kicked his leg out to sweep Grier's knees as

Fiona came downstairs in a robe that barely hid the nightie beneath. Black ribbons held the lace together and Grier had a compelling urge to block her from Tyler's view. But since he was still on the ground, face hovering just above the carpet with Tyler's knee in his back, nothing much he could do.

"What the hell is going on down here?" She looked at the furniture knocked askew then glared from Grier to Tyler. "And what the hell are you doing here?"

"Came to sweep your place as we discussed this afternoon."

She crossed her arms as Tyler stood and Grier made it to his feet. "A little late for that now, don't you think?" She rolled her eyes. "I see you've met my husband."

Grier swiped the back of his hand over his busted lip. "You hired him for security?"

She turned to him all icy anger. "Well, I've spent so much time alone lately."

His fault? She'd found a way to make hiring this asshat Grier's fault? She had to be kidding. But there was nothing playful in her glare. Nothing that said she was the same woman who wanted him in her bed not ten minutes earlier. "I'm here now."

She rolled her eyes, scoffed even. "But leaving as soon as we finish, no doubt."

Grier shook his head, shamed she could read him.

His skin had to be fifty shades of embarrassed. "Can we not do this in front of this guy?"

"You're shy now?"

If that fucker said one more word, Grier would be happy to chime the bell for round two.

"Go home, Grier. Wherever it is, we both know you never planned it to be here." Her voice dropped, and she wouldn't lift her gaze to look at him.

And damned if he could figure out what happened in the last ten minutes that made her so sad.

12

*G*rier was MIA again. He'd gone on overnight runs, multi-state runs to escort cargo, and he'd taken to speaking to her through Sage. Not that she didn't like Sage, he was okay as far as guys who weren't Grier went, but dammit, she hadn't married Sage. Hadn't been given a year to make a baby with Sage.

Tyler popped a hip onto the corner of her desk. "What's up today, boss lady?"

She pulled papers from under his ass, crinkled papers now, and smoothed them with her hand before shoving them into a folder. "Couple of deliveries tonight. We'll need to make sure the boys are in the yard. Four for each truck."

Usually, as soon as she spoke, he beelined to carry out her orders. Now he sat as comfortable as if she'd provided an easy chair with a remote control and a cold beer. "Your husband's back."

He'd been back a hundred times. Left a hundred, too. "So?"

"Does that mean I'm sleeping on the back porch so you and lover boy can have a reunion special in the house?" His smirk said he knew the answer.

She'd been meaning to speak to him about their "living" arrangements. "You don't have to stay anymore. I think the worst is passed. The guys seem okay now."

"Yeah. The dissension in the ranks seems to have dissipated." He picked up a pen and twirled it between his fingers. "Were you really worried about one of your own men trying to take you down?"

She wasn't going to tell him her real motives for having him there. No reason to.

As she sat pretending to ignore him, he reached to brush her hair back from her forehead. "Fiona, you're too young and beautiful to be stuck in some dead-end marriage to a guy who'd rather leave you home alone every night than make you feel like his woman." He stood and pulled her against him. He smelled like exhaust fumes and cologne. "If you were mine…"

"Cozy."

The voice came from the doorway, a voice Fiona missed. She pushed Tyler away and sat back in her chair.

Tyler smiled down at her. "I'll go tell Nate about tonight."

She nodded and cleared her throat as he smirked and walked past Grier.

The bags under Grier's eyes spoke to his late nights. "I gotta say, babe. You can do better. Your boyfriend is skeevy."

"And my husband doesn't want me." The words burned in her throat. Not as much as his barely veiled accusation. He sat in the chair across her desk and stared at her until she felt the urge to squirm. "He's not my boyfriend." Grier cocked an eyebrow. "If he was, would you be jealous?"

Oh, God. Why had she asked that? The answer had the potential to kill her. Either way.

"I don't share."

Wasn't that a joke. "You'd have to have had me to share me."

"You're my wife." His voice was low. Dangerous. The Grier she remembered from long ago.

"Convenient of you to remember." If she sounded bitter, which she did, he was the one to blame. All she'd wanted was a few nights with happy endings, maybe a baby, and he'd ruined it all. Smashed her dreams like he'd smashed her TV.

"Oh, Fifi. I never forgot."

She sighed. On an ordinary day, she wouldn't have

asked, wouldn't have cared, but she hadn't slept in what felt like months. "Why'd you marry me, Grier?"

"Why'd you bring me back here?"

"To marry me. Ironic, huh?" She chuckled, but there was nothing funny about this.

"What is?"

And oh, for the love of God. Did he really have to use that soft, sweet tone? The one he'd used to comfort her after Max died? It made hating him difficult. "On that flight to Belize, I hated you. I'd told Max you were the only one I would consider, but I knew. No way would I go through with it." She shook her head, unable and maybe unwilling to stop now. "I had this fantasy about us when I was younger. And I really thought I outgrew it. But then you came walking out of that gate, confident and so sure of yourself. I was seventeen again. I might have actually heard the wedding march in my head, maybe I even saw myself in the white dress with you waiting for me, so happy to be with me." She shook her head and rolled her eyes. "If I'd known being married to you would be like this, I probably would have readjusted my fantasy."

"Probably?"

"Don't do that." Every time he spoke in that deep, sexy tone, a part of her hoped he meant it. A part of her wanted it to mean something more than it did.

"Do what?"

"I'm not a toy, Grier. And I lose everything if we get divorced, which I won't do, but we don't have to pretend." He stared at her or through her, she couldn't tell. Nor did she care. She just wanted to put an end to the hope that rang through her every time she heard a bike on the street outside her townhouse.

"What about the baby?"

Funny. She'd never wanted one so badly before until she knew she wouldn't be having one. And it wasn't about the money, either. It was more. Things she couldn't describe or find words for. Emotions she didn't know she had.

"The will said I had to have a baby in a year. It didn't say it had to be yours."

"I think it was implied."

"Well, that offer isn't on the table."

"Again, I don't share." At some point, he'd moved around the desk to stand beside her and spin her chair toward him. He braced one hand on each of the armrests and leaned in. "Close your eyes, Fiona."

"Why?" She wasn't afraid of him, but he hadn't given her any reason to trust him either.

"Just do it." She stared, wishing she had the power to read his mind. "Please?"

She complied. "Okay. Now what?"

"Picture us in ten years, or five, with a kid. We aren't

exactly living our best lives here. Is this what you want for a kid?"

Oh, she'd seen that picture before a thousand times in her mind. She didn't even have to close her eyes anymore to see it. "It was good enough for me."

"Was it now?" He straightened.

"No one in my life has meant more to me than Max." She shook her head. "And Belize is better?"

"Safer."

"I don't know. I've heard some pretty bad things about jellyfish." She shook her head. Enough of this already. She'd spent a week wondering whether or not she would have to visit a sperm bank. At least now she knew. Knowing meant acceptance would come. She sighed. "Look, Grier. I can't divorce you or I lose everything. But I won't make you be a part of the baby situation. I can handle that on my own." The baby situation? She hated herself for thinking the words.

"We'll see."

She didn't let the hope bud inside of her, wouldn't let him make her his emotional yo-yo. He'd made his decision, and now she'd made hers. "No. We won't. The baby will be mine. I don't need you for that."

And no matter what he said or what he did, she'd decided.

* * *

GODDAMMIT. Shit. Grier slammed his hand against the hood of the Suburban in the garage. The same Suburban he'd been sleeping in these last weeks while that son of a bitch Sedotal slept down the hall from Fiona, or worse, with her. He picked up a wrench from the toolbox open at his side and spun to throw it at the wall. "Fuck!" The picture in his mind caused a physical ache in his chest.

Sage opened the door and shut it as a screwdriver came screaming through the air toward him and stuck in the door at eye level. He opened the door again and stepped through. "Bad day?"

Understatement. Grier picked up another screwdriver and didn't aim but hit a blond on a poster hanging over the workbench along the opposite wall. If Fiona slept with that… Sedotal, Grier would kill him.

Sage leaned against the SUV. "Two trucks coming in tonight. You going?"

Of course, he was going. His wife had a boyfriend. Living with her. What else was Grier going to do? He looked at his buddy. "What do you know about Sedotal?"

"Nothing that makes me damage calendar girls with screwdrivers. And probably not more than you do." He shrugged. "He doesn't talk to us except to spew orders from Fiona. Spends all his time following her around…" As if a lightbulb switched on in his head. "Oh!" He handed Grier another screwdriver. "All this anger and aggression makes sense now."

"Where's he from?"

Sage shook his head. "I don't know. He never said."

"How did he meet Fiona?"

Sage picked up a pair of pliers and fiddled with the handle. "I heard she picked him up from the prison when he got out."

"Did she know him before prison or did someone arrange this?" Someone had to have introduced them. Fiona wasn't the kind of girl who hung around prisons looking to fill staff vacancies. When he'd known her before, she was the kind of girl who hung around Starbucks. Now, honestly, he couldn't say. Didn't know that and a hell of a lot more about his wife.

"I don't know."

"Can you find out?" If anyone could, it was Sage. He talked when he needed, but more he was the strong silent type who knew how to blend in and listen.

"He's security. I'm security. I can take him out for a beer or ten, get him talking."

Grier nodded. "Thanks. I owe you one."

"Why the sudden interest?"

Sudden wasn't quite the right word. "He's been staying with Fiona." He shook his head. "As her protection." And he'd just become one of those guys who used air quotes. God, he hated those guys.

"Well, you're not."

Grier shot him a scowl.

"Dude, they have pills. Just swallow your pride and—"

"I don't need fucking pills." Damn her. Damn Sedotal. Damn the little blue pills. Damn it all.

"They aren't just for fucking."

Grier threw up his hands. He needed a drink. Something strong. And now.

* * *

"Hello?" Even groggy, her voice turned him on. Maybe because he was picturing her in that damned black robe and whatever lacy thing she'd been hiding underneath it.

"Hey, baby." If his words slurred, it was probably because he hadn't slept well for days. Weeks. Since the first time he'd seen her again, sat next to her on the plane and first inhaled her perfume. Or maybe it was the tequila. Probably the tequila.

"Grier?"

Oh, the way she said his name. "I don't want you to sleep with Sedotal. I don't want you to have anyone else's baby." He wanted her to have his baby, dammit.

"Are you drunk?" Her voice shrilled between cell towers and landed in his ear.

"No." He sighed. He didn't want to lie to her. "Yeah. But I wasn't drunk four hours ago, and I didn't want you to sleep with him then either."

"Grier, I'm going back to bed. You should, too."

"Can I come over?" God. He sounded desperate. "I just want to see you."

"Go to bed."

"Fiona, wait." He could still hear her breathing on the line. "I want to take back all the things I said. Not tonight. I meant that. Don't sleep with him." Oh, God. What if Sedotal was lying beside Fiona now? "Is *he* there?"

"No. I told him I don't need him to stay here anymore."

"Good." Unless she'd already slept with him. "Did you guys…?"

"Goodbye, Grier." She hung up.

Well, that hadn't gone the way he'd hoped. Damn the tequila filling him with stupid ideas that he could have her and their baby and the life he'd always wanted.

He carried his bottle of tequila out to the parking lot behind the clubhouse and fell onto the grass. Maybe tonight he'd be able to sleep.

13

Fiona rolled over. Nothing but a cold pillow on the other side. No husband, though she had one. No man to keep her warm, though she should have been able to find one. Thunder cracked outside and the rain beat against the window in a steady thrum. A perfect day to snuggle up in bed and watch movies or… not watch movies.

But not for the woman who had a thousand responsibilities to a motorcycle club with shipments to deliver and money to collect. She threw off the blanket and stood, glad for once she'd gone back to pajama pants and old t-shirts for sleeping. The lingerie she'd bought for Grier sat dry-rotting in her underwear drawer since she'd woken up and bumped into Tyler Sedotal in the bathroom. His gaze, it had felt more like a leer, made her uncomfortable, and she hadn't been looking for a repeat performance.

Coffee. She wanted some. Maybe because she smelled it brewing and knew she hadn't set the timer last night. Because she'd wanted to sleep in this morning, and she liked the just brewed taste rather than the couple-hours-old bite. She opened the drawer next to the bed and slid the .22 her father had given her from the nightstand drawer.

She held it in her left hand and wrapped her right hand around the bottom of the handle just the way Max had shown her. Steady. Strong. Fearless. Nary a tremble. Back against the wall, she edged down the steps as silent as if she still slept. She peeked around the wall as she came down the steps. She could see a black boot, a knee clad in blue denim. Who the hell would break in to sit at her table and drink coffee? No one. But Tyler would let himself in, make himself right at home. She lowered the gun to her side and walked into her kitchen as if she wasn't just ready to end someone.

When she saw him, she stopped. Closed her eyes, rubbed them to make sure they weren't playing with her, then opened them. Still Grier. His hair hung in damp strands over the collar of his leather jacket, and he smiled when he saw her. "Good morning, sleepy."

She set the gun on the table, just to let him know she had it, then went to the coffee maker and poured a cup.

It wasn't until she sat across from him that she really looked at him, past the grassy green eyes, the hint of beard that was either meant to be sexy or meant he was too lazy to buy a razor. She decided on sexy.

"What are you doing here?"

"Woke up passed out in a field." He said it as if it was no big deal.

Since she couldn't decide how or if his answer explained his presence, she concentrated on the fact he'd rather sleep in a field than with her. Even coffee wouldn't help her angry disposition now. She shoved her mug away and crossed her arms. The glare she shot him didn't affect him more than to elicit a smile. "Marriage make you an alcoholic?" Not that he'd acted much like he was married since Max's funeral.

"Not at all." He ran his finger around the lip of his mug. Fiona couldn't tear her gaze away. "Last night, the trucks got hit. There were men waiting on both routes." He leaned back in his chair and crossed his legs, that damned finger still circling the mug. "Nate found Hamilton and Frank this morning. Neither one could say what happened."

"They didn't know?"

"Broken jaws."

And still that damned finger… This time, though, she looked away. Hamilton, her best friend, with a broken jaw.

"Who?" She watched him and his non-reaction said more than anything else he might have spoken. "You have an idea?"

He kept his face blank, and dammit, she couldn't read him. "No."

Yes, he did. The flicker in his eye said he wasn't quite comfortable lying. Damned if she planned to tell him. "Where are they?"

"Ham is with Jez now. Frank's at home." He straightened. "What about the other truck?"

"Empty. Burned. Driver's missing."

Shit. That shipment, and the other, were meant for a new client. Someone they would lose. "What about the riders escorting the second truck?"

"Your boyfriend got a little roughed up. Said he didn't see anything until the car ran them off the road. He passed out. Has some road rash, a couple of black eyes." Grier stood. "Don't worry. I'm sure he'll be back tonight." He watched her face, tried measuring her. Frowned when she showed nothing. "For you."

His mouth twitched as he clenched his jaw. So he could almost hide a lie, but the jealousy on his face was as bright as a beacon.

She nodded, pleased with all she'd learned. "Good to know." But she'd told Tyler to put four men on each truck. So far, she'd heard about three total. "What about the others?"

He listed the casualties. "Jez is taking care of them."

The missing shipments would be a problem. A big one. She needed to get on the phone and do some damage control. "I need to get on this."

He nodded but didn't move. "Sage is on it with your boyfriend."

Boyfriend. That was the second time. She waited.

"Are you seeing him?" She didn't answer, continued watching him. He clenched his fist. "Are you fucking him?"

"Do you care?" He looked down and relaxed his hand. "Do. You. Care?"

Grier stood and walked to the French doors that led to her back yard. "I asked first." He shook his head. "And I know. I don't deserve an answer. I just… want one." The way his voice dropped sent shivers over her skin. Shoulder to toe.

"You don't want me. What do you care?" She kept her tone hard. Ignored the ping in her chest.

"Don't want you." He scoffed. "I wish that was true." He continued speaking to the window. "I want you so bad I can't think. I can't sleep. I think about you… all the time."

Lies. Had to be. Especially since she was his wife. "And yet, I've been here every single night alone."

"But not alone, right? Your boyfriend stays here."

"He's not my boyfriend. And he stays here because

my husband would rather be anywhere else than here." She spoke softly because saying the words caused a physical pain in her throat. A tightness that made it hard to even breathe.

Grier turned. "Fiona." He crossed to her, stood less than a breath away, hands at his side, eyes searching hers.

The decision was hers. He'd given her that. Instead of moving closer or kissing him, she reached for his belt, unfastened the buckle, and slid the black leather through the loops, pulling it free. She waited for his half-smile before she went after the button. He took her hand. "Let's lock the door this time."

As he walked away, she pulled his phone from his back pocket. "And let's shut these off." No phone call would rob her of the moment she'd been waiting for since she was a teenager. She tossed the phone on the sofa.

He flipped the deadbolt and turned to her. "God, you're beautiful." This time he tangled his fingers in her hair and pulled until their lips crashed together. His mouth, as hot and hard as his body, caressed hers, made promises, turned her whimper into a full-on moan. She let her hands dance over his chest, felt the firm cord of muscles and sinew under her palms. A hundred times she'd seen him without a shirt, imagined what it would be like to touch him while he wanted her instead of forcing herself on him.

She anchored one hand at the back of his neck and held on when he slipped his tongue in her mouth. Her world shifted and there was only Grier. His hands on her skin. His mouth on hers. His dick was hard and ready as he lifted her. She wrapped her legs around him and held on as he carried her up the stairs, never breaking the kiss.

He brought her into the bedroom, and she slid down the front of him until her feet touched the floor before she looked up at him. Her desire exploded, stole her breath. Never had a man looked at her with such intensity, made her feel so wanted. Warmth spread through her as she stared at him.

This moment lived up to its hype, to every dream and fantasy she'd ever had about Grier. He smiled. "Remember when I told you to change into something sexy for me?"

Oh yeah. She remembered. She nodded.

"If I ever tell you that again, this—" He wagged his finger in front of her. "—is what I want you to wear."

She smiled. "You think you're going to tell me how to dress?"

"Oh, baby, that's the least of the things I'm going to tell you to do." He stepped closer, lifted the hem of her shirt, and ran his finger back and forth over her stomach. Her skin burned.

"Yeah? You think so?" That wasn't the plan at all. She would be giving the orders, taking control, showing him who was the boss.

He pulled her in closer. "I know so." His touch burned. His gaze smoldered. And she took in everything, every breath, the slightest touch, the fire in his eyes. "You're going to do exactly what I say and you're going to want to do it."

"Wanna bet?" She would wager everything she owned that, by the end of the night, she would have him wrapped around her little finger. Such a waste of time standing here bantering when they could be on the bed fucking.

"Breakfast in bed?"

She grinned. "I like my eggs scrambled."

"And I like my bacon crisp." He kissed her, softly, a feather over her lips. When he pulled away, she strained to reach him. He spun her around so her back was against his chest. His mouth trailed from her earlobe to her shoulder while he cupped and massaged her breast with one hand and slipped the other into her pajama pants. "Somebody forgot their panties this morning."

She would have answered but he slipped a finger between her wet folds, swiped it over her clit, then pushed back inside her. Her breath rushed out in a gasp.

"You like that?" He nibbled her neck as his finger pumped in and out. There was only Grier. The rest of the world ceased to exist. She twisted her shoulders, wanting, needing to kiss him, but she couldn't move far enough, and his hold tightened.

"Grier, kiss me."

"No." He withdrew his touch, left her cold and shivering, hot and burning. "Don't turn around."

He could play his game, and she'd go along for a minute. Until her head cleared at least. She waited, listening to the furniture, her mirror, moving and the water running in the bathtub, his footsteps going down then coming up the steps. Still, she didn't move.

* * *

So many fantasies. So many nights he'd spent picturing Fiona. And tonight, he would make all those fantasies come true.

"Come here." He stood at the edge of her bed. The bath had been run, a steaming bath that would be cold if he didn't get her in there soon, but he needed to look at her, to see her gray eyes go stormy, to watch her lip quiver just before he kissed her, to hear the little moans in the back of her throat when he touched her. Right now, he needed to savor Fiona. His wife. The way he should have all these weeks.

137

She turned and walked toward him, more accurately stalked toward him. Her smile, one of the sexiest things he'd ever seen, radiated toward him. "Is the bath for you or for me?"

He grinned because not to grin would have just been silly. "It's for us."

"Are we getting dirty?"

This woman. Every single thing from her feigned innocence to the color of her toenail polish, including her plaid pajama pants, turned him on and made his dick throb with need. "God, I hope so."

She slid her hands underneath his shirt, pushing the light black fabric up. When he lifted his arms, she pulled it over his head. "Well, let's see what we can do to make that happen." She ran a fingernail down the center of his chest, circling his belly button.

He didn't throw her onto the bed, didn't kiss her. Instead, he concentrated on standing still, waiting, breathing slowly because hyperventilating right now would have been damned inconvenient, as inconvenient as his conscience. He put a hand on each of her shoulders. "Fiona. Are you sure?"

She nodded without hesitation or even taking a second to think about it. "I've been sure for a really..." She flicked open the button on his jeans. "Long..." Her fingers fumbled with the zipper but she lowered it, and he closed his eyes to savor the sensation of her hand against his cock. "Time."

Her eyes darkened as he lifted her and carried her to the bed. He laid her in the center then braced a hand on each side of her. This wasn't his plan. He'd planned to make her beg, make her want him in ways she didn't know she wanted him. And if he didn't get this moving soon, he was going to be the one begging.

He kissed her, moving slowly and languidly, as if he wasn't about to spontaneously combust, and his heart went wild when she wrapped her hand around him and stroked. "Tell me what you want, Grier."

Everything. He wanted every damned thing she had to offer. "I want you to take that shirt off and those pants." When she smiled but didn't move, he lowered his head as if to kiss her and whispered, "Now."

Back on track. More so when she stood and tossed her clothes away. He had to do it this way or their night would end way too soon.

"Come back to bed now." She slid onto the bed next to him, and he turned to prop himself on an elbow and look down at her. "Don't move." He loved her confidence, that she didn't try to hide herself no matter how intense he stared. How he'd managed to resist this woman for so much as an hour and why he'd tried at all seemed almost crazy.

He cupped her breast and rolled her nipple between

his finger and thumb. Her sharp intake of breath turned into a full-on gasp moan combo when he took the tight bud into his mouth and swirled his tongue around and around. She arched her back, and he slid his hand down her stomach then… lower.

"Lie still." He slipped another finger inside her and she lifted her hips and raised a hand as if she wanted to touch him. Fuck. He would come undone if she touched him, lose any control he had left. "No, Fiona." She lowered her hand and whimpered.

His heart hammered pushing all the blood to his throbbing cock. He wanted to be inside her and needed to feel the wet heat of her pussy around his dick.

"You want more?" He withdrew his hand then pushed in hard. Everything was so tight, so wet. He lowered his head and pulled her nipple into his mouth, sucking, licking, teasing and soothing. She moaned and shifted so her hips were closer. He wanted to put his head between her legs and taste her, but it would have to wait. Right now, he needed to be inside her, needed to see her face as she came, hear her call out for him. "Ask me to fuck you, Fiona."

"No."

He sucked harder. Rolled her nipple between his teeth as his tongue flicked side to side. He withdrew his fingers. He had to get rid of these jeans. Had to bury himself inside her before his body exploded. He stood.

Pushed his pants down and stepped out. Watched as Fiona touched herself, as her long fingers disappeared into her pussy. He stroked his cock as she pleased herself, using one hand inside and the other to rub her clit.

Oh, God. She was hot. Erotic hot. Fucking hottest women he'd ever seen. "Watch me, Grier."

"Don't come." He wanted to be inside her when she came, wanted to feel that perfect pussy squeeze his dick. "I mean it. If you come now, without me, I will tease you all night long and make you wait until tomorrow morning." Her every breath came with a moan, and he knew she was close. "Ask me now, Fiona."

"Fuck me, Grier." He took her wrist and slid her fingers out of her pussy then brought them to his lips and sucked the juice off. He loved the tangy salty taste of her, loved more the way her eyelids fluttered shut when he used the tip of his cock to rub her opening. "Oh, God, please."

And when she put it like that… Slick heat wrapped around his cock, and he groaned. He started slow, watching her face, feeling her muscles contract as she met him thrust for thrust. Her hands clawed his back and his cocked throbbed with need and lust and desire. And it turned out he loved watching her. He rolled them so she was on top. "Show me what you want, Fiona."

She guided his hands to her breasts as she rode his

dick. His eyes blurred and his head spun. He was too close, too… oh, God. She arched her back, put her hands behind her, braced them on his thighs and the angles… the view… when she ground her hips hard against him and a deep guttural moan escaped her throat, he let go. He couldn't stop. His hips bucked and he sat up to wrap his arms around her, pushing deeper, as deep as he could go. Where he belonged.

14

Fiona watched him sleep. A shock of hair fell over his forehead. When she'd first seen him, the too-long hair had bothered her, but now, after watching him flip it back, tie it away from his face, swipe it over to one side, she didn't want to imagine him without it.

"Watching a guy sleep is kind of creepy." He spoke with his eyes still closed but a half-smile on his lips. "You're not planning my death, are you?"

She rested her chin on the back of her hands over his chest. "Not yet."

"Oh good." He folded his arm under his head. "You owe me breakfast."

Yes, she did. He'd delivered everything he promised and more. Unfortunately, she'd never learned to cook and her part of town didn't have a take-out breakfast place. "Sorry, stud. I don't think I can move." They'd worked out every muscle she owned through the night, and she ached in all the best ways. But when he cupped her breast and teased her nipple between his fingers, she slithered up to kiss him. "That is not going to make me want to get out of bed."

He rolled them over and rested his weight on his elbows. "Breakfast can wait." He kissed her again, soft at first, then harder, more passionate until her blood thrummed through her and her stomach clenched. Her phone rang, and she reached for it as Grier took her nipple into his mouth. "Don't answer it."

But she'd already pressed the green button. "Hello."

"Fiona, it's Sage. We lost another shipment last night."

Thanks to Grier and his magical tongue, it took a minute before Sage's words registered. "How?"

Sage sighed, and Fiona stifled a moan as Grier made a production of lowering the blanket and pouring a few drops of warming massage gel on her clit. Sage might as well have been talking to himself for all the listening she did. "Oh, God."

"It'll be okay. I'll take Grier and Tyler out to do some research in town. Don't worry, Fiona. We'll figure this out." He paused. "Have you seen Grier? He didn't stay at the club last night and his phone is going straight to voicemail." Because she'd turned it off. He didn't let her answer before he continued. "Anyway, if you see Grier, tell him I'm looking for him, would you?"

"Uh-huh." She dropped the phone over the side of the bed. The shipment had already been stolen. No reason to… Oh, God. Pressure built inside her. Glorious pressure. Grier kissed her hard, and she wanted more. More of him. And like every time she'd wanted him inside her last night, he made her ask. "Please, can I have your dick?"

He rolled onto his back. "Come get it."

She threw one leg over him and lowered herself onto his cock. His hands came around to knead her ass. "Don't move yet. I want to enjoy this view first."

His dick twitched inside of her, and she bit her lip to keep from crying out. The combination of the warming gel—he'd found her secret supply on a shelf in the bathroom when they'd gotten out of the shower last night—and his dick brought her so close to the edge she teetered toward release.

He'd told her he liked to watch her so she didn't wait for him to command her to touch her tits. His eyes darkened and he sat up, using one hand behind him for leverage as he bucked his hips and she met each stroke of his cock inside her. Her body tightened, and she stopped moving. He hadn't told her it was okay to come yet. And there were penalties—okay, totally hot penalties that she didn't really mind—for coming before he "allowed" it.

He moaned as she ground her hips. "Are you ready, baby?"

"God, yes." She barely got the words out before her body shattered.

"Oh, God, Fiona!" His voice, deep, low, guttural, shot through her along with the aftershocks she'd come to love. She collapsed on top of him and worked to catch her breath while he rubbed her back and murmured words too soft for her to hear.

When she finally rolled away, Grier stood and disappeared into the bathroom. The shower came on and his off-key singing rang through her room. If she had one ounce of energy left, she would have joined him. But moving wasn't on her morning agenda more than snuggling into her blanket, smelling Grier's cologne on her pillow, and falling back to sleep before she had to get up to deal with stolen shipments and bad security.

* * *

SLEEPING with Fiona had been something akin to a religious experience. There had certainly been a lot of *oh, God* going on in her room—uh, their room? But in the harsh light of day, nothing between them had changed.

And they had bigger problems than which side of the bed they should each take—not that they'd talked about him coming back or staying. Which he wouldn't. Shouldn't. Would decide about later.

As he climbed on his bike, he pulled out his phone and dialed Sage. Sage had barely managed to get out "Hello" before Grier started with, "What the hell happened to those shipments?"

"Fiona took our guns, and we can't defend the shipments against guys who are allowed to carry theirs." He sighed. "You gotta talk to her. Explain. I know she wants to do things differently to Max, make it more above board, but we're out-manned and out-gunned."

"Yeah." Sending the guys out without a way to protect themselves from whichever club had gone raider was dangerous. Grier didn't want to undermine her authority. God knew she was having enough trouble holding onto it on her own. He'd heard the talk. "Okay. Anybody who transports or escorts can carry their weapons." He'd deal with Fiona later. Right now, he needed to figure out what to do about the shipments they'd lost. "I'll be there in a few. We need to go find out who has our shit and get it back."

"I'll get Tyler."

The last thing Grier wanted was Sedotal around. "No. You and me." And so Sage didn't question him, he added, "Two is just a couple of buddies out riding. Three is a club on the hunt. Leave him and meet me at the South Street Diner."

Sage hung up, and Grier started the bike. No way would he let the club go down. This was important to Fiona and that made it important to him. He'd decide why later.

"Fiona doesn't seem like the kind of woman who's going to put up with you banging somebody else." Sage sipped his coffee, even blew on the rim as he stared at Grier.

"What are you talking about?"

"Well, shipments are missing, it's the asscrack of dawn and you're smiling like a fool and snarfing down enough food to feed the crowd at St. Francis House. It doesn't take a genius to figure out somebody got laid. It also doesn't take a genius to know Fiona's going to kill you when she finds out." He reached for a piece of bacon and Grier smacked his hand away.

"I've got Fiona under control. Don't worry your pretty little head." Grier smiled. Fiona. She'd been in bed when he left, a contented smile on her lips, and hopefully a sweet dream about him in her head.

"I'm just saying. Since Hamilton is out of commission, she'll probably have her new boy toy shoot you in your sleep."

"New boy toy?" Grier stared. What the hell had Sage heard? Probably the same things he had. Probably that Sedotal was making up for *all* the things Grier hadn't been doing.

Sage looked down and pursed his lips. "I don't know if it's true, but some of the guys are talking. And while you've been staying at the club, he's been at her place." He smiled up at the waitress when she stopped to refill his cup.

It gave Grier a minute to think. Fiona. His woman. His wife. And he'd neglected her. If she had screwed Sedotal, he couldn't blame her. Damned sure he could blame that fucker though.

"And she gave him your bike."

Grier snapped his head up. "She did what?" He'd been riding an old Harley they'd restored at the club-house. A spare. Because Fiona hadn't given him back the one he'd spent months restoring with Max. And now Sedotal was riding Grier's bike?

Sage cleared his throat. "He rode it in this morning. Said she wanted him to have it. Made it sound like… payment for services ren… dered…"

The murderous rage pumping through Grier and the look it likely inspired probably had something to do with the way Sage let his words fall off. Grier stood, threw some money on the table, and stalked out to his borrowed bike.

Sage followed him out of the diner, but Grier was already on the bike, racing toward the clubhouse.

* * *

EVERYTHING GRIER SAW as he drove was tinged in a homicidal red. He was going to paint the walls with Sedotal's blood. First, for riding his bike, and second, for riding his wife. Or maybe the order was reversed. It didn't matter. It was going to get messy.

He drove into the lot, pulled in front of the shop, and got off the bike. Sedotal had a wrench in his hand and bike parts strewn from the near bay where he'd disassembled Grier's bike to the opposite end of the shop. Grier didn't give a shit about the wrench or the crowd of Demons standing around in bunches. He only saw Sedotal and what was left of his ride. And red. A lot of red.

The first punch knocked Sedotal down. The second —the one that came with Grier on top of him—knocked out Sedotal's tooth and split Grier's knuckle open. Blood spurted as he hit Sedotal again and again until Sage, One-eye, and Hamilton yanked him off.

He fought to get around Hamilton. "You're out of here, you stupid fuck."

Sage had one arm trapped behind him, Nate the other, and Hamilton stood directly in front with a hand on Grier's chest, blocking his path to finishing the job of killing Sedotal, who remained on the ground.

He couldn't actually kick him out. Didn't have the power for that. It would take a vote. If Sedotal had been a Demon. But he wasn't. He was bought and paid for security. Who didn't know when to keep his mouth shut. Grier tried not to think what else Fiona had been paying him for.

"I was just taking care of *your* business. A woman like Fiona needs a man to keep her warm at night. I was helping out. Not my fault she enjoyed it and wanted more." He'd barely made it to standing—no one helping him made it take a couple of extra seconds—when Grier broke free and knocked him back onto his ass. Out cold.

Grier jerked away again when Hamilton—a mountain of a man with the strength of two—grabbed him in a bear hug and part lifted, part dragged him out of the shop. "Put me down."

Hamilton dropped him outside in the parking lot. He still looked awful and had a wire around the lower half of his face, but fierce as ever, he pointed at Grier. "Stay."

"Fuck you, Hamilton." But he looked down at his bleeding hand. Every knuckle had been busted open, and he was pretty sure he'd broken at least one finger, but aside from Fiona, nothing in his life had been more satisfying as hearing the thwack of his fist against Sedotal's face, of seeing blood fly, and feeling the son of a bitch's nose break.

Hamilton provided a wall between him and the shop, and One-eye came with Sage to block Grier in. "She gave him the bike, Grier."

He couldn't think about Fiona now or he would explode. Blood dripped down his fingers, and his hand throbbed, but damned if he wanted to stay there with the whole club thinking Sedotal had been doing his woman. Their leader.

He climbed on the bike and rode. Past Salem, through Gloucester to Rockport and the beach where he'd watched Fiona clock a guy who got handsy with her when she'd convinced him to let her skip school her senior year in high school. Even then, in the black and red bikini with the silver trim—the inspiration for paint colors on his bike—she'd made his dick hard. And now, he had no bike, and she'd added Sedotal to her list of conquests. And there had to have been several. That woman knew exactly how to get him off. Not that he had any right to judge. Wasn't like he'd come home a virgin, but dammit, to be screwing Sedotal now, while she was married to Grier… unforgivable.

The beach was deserted except for Grier and a few people walking, picking up shells, and mocking his life with their happiness. He'd stopped in Gloucester for a bottle of whiskey. He hadn't opened it yet, but the picture of Sedotal on top of Fiona kept flashing through his mind, along with one of her handing him the keys to Grier's bike, and a particularly hurtful one of her fucking that piece of shit on Grier's bike. He twisted the cap and drank, long and deep, hoping to numb the pain, quiet the voices—*I was taking care of your business*—and dim the pictures.

By sunset, he was pleasantly drunk and not angry—not *as* angry—at Fiona for giving his bike away to that loser. He was still furious about her screwing the guy though. And no amount of whiskey was going to make that go away. She'd made him a fool. A laughingstock. For Tyler Sedotal, a guy who couldn't take a punch, who should've hit Grier with the wrench before he ever got close enough to nail him with a fist. A guy who tore Grier's bike apart.

He pulled out his cell and turned the power back on. He had about a thousand missed calls and texts to deal with, but nothing was more important than setting things straight with Fiona. Giving her a piece of his mind. His hand, swollen now to twice its original size and caked with blood and sand was all but useless in trying to work the phone. It took a couple of tries before he managed to dial her number.

"Grier. Where are you?"

"What? No hello for your husband?" Though still

sitting on the beach, he swayed as he spoke. "Do you save all the sweet stuff for Sedotal?"

"Look, One-eye told me what happened with you and Ty."

Oh, Ty was it? "You gave him my bike."

"To wash it and tune it up. It's been sitting for two years. I wanted to give it back to you." He didn't care how reasonable it sounded. He didn't believe her.

"Bullshit."

"It's true, and I don't care what you think." Even drunk, he could hear her defiance.

"Barbie wouldn't talk to Ken that way. And if she did, he'd turn her over his knee." What? Since when was he an expert on five-year-old girl toys? "Anyway, you need a spanking. A nice hard swat against that luscious ass." He couldn't keep his thoughts straight. He went from angry to horny in one point five seconds flat.

She chuckled. "Where are you, Grier?"

"Out." He pictured her as he left her, naked and smiling. "What are you wearing, Fifi?"

She paused. "Jeans and a tank top."

"Are you in your office?" Not that it mattered. But he wanted to be able to imagine her.

"Yeah."

"Is the door shut?"

He heard her heels clicking on the floor. "It is now."

"Good." Even as drunk as he'd ever been in his life,

this woman had the power to make his cock hard from fifty miles away. "Touch yourself for me."

Oh, God. He wished he had one of those phones with video chat capabilities. He closed his eyes. Why hadn't he'd gotten a hotel where he could rub one off while she filled his ears with her sultry voice describing things he had vivid mental imagery now to go with? Better yet, he wished he was in her office with her, bending her over the desk, sliding into her from behind.

"I'm at work, Grier."

"You're the one who shut the door, Fi. You want this. You know you do." He didn't know more for certain than it was what he wanted. "Are you touching yourself?"

"Yes." His heart lurched at her whisper and his cock threatened to explode.

"Is your pussy wet?" He imagined it, slick and glistening, and licked his lips.

"Yes."

"What do you want, Fiona?" She didn't answer with more than a moan. "Tell me what you want."

"I want you to come home and fuck me." Each word, punctuated by a pant, threatened any control not already voided by the whiskey.

"Mm." He closed his eyes. This place was too public to touch himself, but his hand curled into a fistful of sand. His brain, what wasn't mush from the alcohol, produced a picture of Tyler Sedotal, face bruised and bloody, holding Fiona's hips as he pounded into her from behind. That bastard. "Call out his name, Fiona."

"What?" She was still panting, her breaths a pulsating breeze in his ear.

"Call out his name." His blood ran cold. His dick went soft. And he sat up.

"What?"

"*Oh, Tyler.* Or do you call him *Ty* when he's inside you?" Rage bubbled under his skin. Jack Daniels' courage had never served him very well. Today wasn't different.

"Fuck you, Grier." She hung up the phone.

Grier stood, launched his phone into the ocean and fell on his face in the sand. It was a fine place to sleep until morning.

15

If Fiona kept a diary of her days, wrote down the events and happenings in her life, the last couple of weeks would all have a single word as their entry—shit. They'd lost a total of six shipments and were no closer to finding out who'd taken them. Grier had gone AWOL, just as she'd known he would. Not AWOL from the club, just from her since she'd hung up on him after he interrupted what could have been an earth-rocking orgasm with his ridiculous accusations. He'd been taking runs and spent whatever free-time he managed putting his bike back together. But when it came time to knock-off for the day, instead of coming home to his wife, he'd gone back to staying in one of the rooms at the clubhouse.

And it made her pathetic. She'd spent one night with him. A glorious night, but a single night. It didn't make sense to miss him so much. So much that keeping her mind focused on work while he spent time in the shop —so close and still so far—where she could watch him, remember, fantasize… made her job impossible. No wonder they'd kept losing shipments.

Sedotal, on the other hand, had gone AWOL. She hadn't seen him since Grier busted up his face. Of course, she'd seen the video from the cameras in the garage. And the one that new kid thought to record on his phone—in color. She'd never seen Grier so angry. Not even when she was younger and a rival club had tried to take out Max.

She walked to the window in her office—the one that looked out into the shop—and stared at Grier's back. She knew every tattoo and scar from collar to waistband because she'd spent a lot of time at this window watching her shirtless husband hunched with a wrench or screwdriver in his hands as he worked to undo what Tyler had done.

Oh, enough already. She flung the office door open and stepped onto the slick concrete in the first work bay. "Grier, we need to talk."

He didn't turn to her. "About what?"

About our marriage. "Shipments." *Coward.*

He turned a ratchet, and the clicks of the metal as he tightened a bolt soothed her. She'd spent about a thousand hours out here when she was a kid. The sights and smells and sounds were the security blanket of her childhood.

"Don't worry about it. I have it taken care of." He tossed the ratchet and stood to wipe the oil from his hands on a blue terry towel he'd had draped across the seat of his bike.

"How?" As club president, she should have been consulted. Informed at least. She narrowed her eyes when he didn't answer. "How?"

He lifted his head and pointed an identical stare at her. "The fewer people who know, the better."

As if he didn't just inspire her to kick his ass, he walked out the open bay door and into the sun. The rays cast a golden halo around his head, and he looked more like an angel than the narcissistic devil she'd decided him to be. She followed him out. He took a beer from a cooler on the table and reclined on the top instead of the bench. "Grier, I demand that you tell me how you have it taken care of."

He leaned on one hand and set the beer to his side so he could use his free hand to nudge her a few steps left. "You're blocking my sun." He laid back and threw an arm over his eyes.

"I'm not leaving until you tell me." By God, he'd have a Fiona sized tan line in the shape of her head across his chest. She sat on the bench, facing out into the parking lot.

"Suit yourself." He didn't move. And by God, neither would she. This was *her* club, *her* job to take care of this, and husband or not, second in command or not, he wouldn't keep secrets from her. The wood creaked as he shifted on the bench. "Fiona."

She wouldn't turn and look at him. Wouldn't gaze up at him like some lovesick puppy. Wouldn't act like anything other than the professional, no-nonsense, intense president of the Screaming Demons Motorcycle Club.

She turned. And gazed. And lifted a hand to lay over his heart.

Warm skin under her palm along with the steady thrum of his heart told her he wasn't as unaffected as he wanted her to believe. And her stomach churned. Bile hitched its way from her stomach to her throat. Now wasn't a good time for the puking. She stood and swayed before Grier's arms came around her, to steady her.

"Fiona?" His concern would have been joyous for Fiona had he not spent two weeks ignoring her. "Are you all right?"

"The flu? I don't know." She couldn't manage more words until she swallowed hard and took a couple of deep, cleansing breaths. The world stopped spinning and her systems settled. "I'm fine." She pushed him off.

Weakness. She hated it. Hated more that she'd just

shown it. Even more that she'd shown it to Grier. She walked on jelly legs away. At least she'd managed to hold her chin up and keep her shoulders back. At that moment, nothing else mattered.

* * *

WHATEVER GRIER HAD DONE, however he was managing, at least they hadn't lost any more shipments over the two weeks since she'd "blocked his sun" outside the shop. Of course, she hadn't seen him either. She worked. She ate. She threw up. She slept. Nothing happened in between. Except for the aching. That happened all the time. Nothing, not warm baths, cold packs, or even sleep, stopped the continuous aching in her back, legs and arms.

"You look like shit."

She didn't deny it. But leave it to Hamilton to point it out.

She shot him a glare. "Thank you. But I can do without your opinion on my appearance."

"Maybe you're working too hard?"

If only he knew that while she showed up at work every day, she spent hours sleeping behind her closed and locked door.

"And maybe I need a vacation, but I have about a thousand things to do." She gestured to the stacks of paper on her desk and blanched when he set a backpack full of this month's "rents" on the towering pile in front of her.

Grumbling under her breath, she stood, turned the dial on the safe once and, if her life depended on it, she wouldn't have been able to tell him or anyone else the combination to the safe. A group of numbers, by the way, she'd known since she was seven. She stared at the dial. Her father's Rolex, his wedding ring, his signed by Elvis Christmas album, and a copy of the family tree lived in that safe. And dammit, she'd forgotten the combination.

"What the fuck…" She held the bag against her chest and sat heavily in the chair. Maybe he was right. She needed rest. A day off. Some time to kick the flu and feel better. She pushed away from the desk and stood, her bed looking better by the minute.

At some point, she would have to deal with the assortment of papers on her desk, but for now, she couldn't think of more than snuggling into her pillow and pretending Grier was there with her. It had worked for a few days, maybe her luck would continue to hold.

GRIER HADN'T SEEN Fiona in three days. Not really seen her in a while. Not held her in longer. And it was killing him. "You going tonight?"

He threw a box down to Sage who caught it and handed it off to Nate who gave it to Frank who piled it with the other boxes in the storage shed. This shipment had electronics that would be picked up to make room for the shipment they were escorting this evening.

Grier stared at Sage. It was either a really big coincidence that since Grier had put his plan in place, not a single shipment had been attacked by whichever band of road pirates had been going after the Demons, or someone had warned them. He didn't want to believe it was Sage, but other than Grier, only Sage knew about the tracking device. He hadn't even told Fiona.

The whistling that always announced Sedotal's arrival made Grier's stomach turn. The last thing he wanted was to deal with that rat bastard, but it turned out, he wasn't there for Grier.

"I'll be right back." Sage walked away with Sedotal, and Grier pretended not to watch them, heads bent together, a lot of nodding from Sedotal. Goddammit. Grier didn't want Sage to be the man on the inside, the one breaking trust, giving away routes and locations. But, while he couldn't say for sure about Sage, he would've bet his left nut Sedotal had a hand in it. He watched for another minute before he climbed down from the truck. "You guys handle tonight? I have stuff to do."

Yeah, he did. Watching them.

Sedotal nodded and reached out a hand. "Look, I wanted to apologize for the shit with your bike and with Fiona." Grier took his hand but didn't buy for a minute that the bastard had an ounce of sincerity in his entire body.

"Yeah. No big deal." Translated: big deal. Very big deal. But Grier nodded. "Let's get this thing unloaded. Like I said..."

Sage chuckled. "Stuff to do."

* * *

THE CAR he'd rented smelled like old men's cologne and sweat. But he couldn't very well roll up on the truck on his bike without being recognized. He didn't even want to power the tinted windows down, but for God's sake... the smell.

The radio played some quiet talk show where the host listened to callers bitch about their lives. To keep from falling asleep waiting for the truck he imagined how his call would go. "Well, I was living the good life down on a private island in Belize when a girl—my one who got away, or more accurately, my girl I was never allowed to have and had to let go—hauled ass through the front gate like she had the devil on her tail. Beautiful. Red-haired. Rage in her eyes. Threatened my friends and said if I came home, she'd leave them on the island, undisturbed and unharmed. And if you knew my girl, you'd know she meant that if I didn't come with her, they would be very disturbed and harmed in ways that would require a medical examiner." So true. Wouldn't have needed a genius or a psychic to read between those lines. Fiona had arrived with murder on her mind. And it was him or Kye. Kye had a woman, a life. Grier had nothing. The decision was easy.

The host would ask some stupid question about whether or not Fiona was the kind of woman he really wanted if she was so dangerous and had to resort to threats to get him to come home. "Hell, yeah. She's everything I ever wanted. Passion and beauty. Intelligence. Sass." He would smile then, picturing her. And boy, did he have some mental memories to choose from. For this, though, he would picture her standing at that gate in Belize, her eyes half-lidded, her hip cocked, and a self-satisfied smile tilting those perfect lips.

He'd go on with the story. Talk about the wedding. Maybe not say it was performed because Max had put a virtual shotgun to his back. And he'd talk about how Fiona, the toughest woman he'd ever met, took the reins at the "company" when her father died.

God, he missed her. More than he would admit to

the host. "I accused her of screwing around. And now, I've ignored her for… too long." The host would ask if Grier really believe Fiona had cheated.

Did he? After all the trouble she's gone to bringing him home, the dangers she'd faced, and every other thing about her—mostly the way she'd responded to him on their one night together—he couldn't believe she would screw Sedotal or anyone else. "No. She didn't cheat."

Saying the words made him question every minute he'd stayed away from her, made his arms ache to hold her, to smell that sweet soft scent of her shampoo as her hair fanned out on the pillow.

As soon as the truck made it to the clubhouse, he was going to drive his rented car straight to Fiona. And speaking of the truck… more than two hours late. Two hours was longer than a flat tire. And someone would have called. He started the car and stared at his phone. No calls, but the app…

He ticked his finger onto the icon and waited for the moving blip to come up. But the little loading wheel continued spinning. No 3G, no 4G, no little half rainbow to tell him he'd connected to some random stranger's WiFi. Fuck! They could have been calling for the last two hours, and he would've never known. He slammed the car into first and laid a strip of rubber on the highway as he took off to find that damned truck.

Less than five miles down the road, two bikes and some of their parts were laid down and scattered along the road. Sage and Sedotal, along the shoulder. He picked them up and sped off. They could get the bikes later. Right now, he needed to find that truck and figure out who the fuck was trying to ruin the Demons' delivery business.

Sage held his head while his arm bled in little bubbles from elbow to wrist. Road rash hurt like hell and Sage's left side was full of it. "What happened?"

Sage looked out the windshield, not at Grier as he spoke. "I don't fucking know. We were riding one in front and one behind, watching like you said, and something... I don't know, blew out the tires on the truck. It swerved. I almost ran up underneath it." Sketchy. And just enough detail to satisfy without giving anything away.

Sedotal leaned forward, a gash on his forehead bleeding like he'd been shot. His eyes had that glassy, concussed look, and had it been anyone else, Grier would've been concerned. But, far as he cared, Sedotal's head could explode.

"I saw the truck in my mirror and turned around. Sage was on the ground, I got hit by something. Put me down, too. We got up and gave chase, but we got maybe two miles and they stopped. We chased ourselves into a trap. They had a line stretched across the road waiting for us."

The truck, a moving van they'd converted, sat on the shoulder another couple of miles down, engulfed in flames. Fucking flames.

Grier couldn't afford to be at the scene when the cops showed up. He banged the palm of his hand against the curve of the steering wheel three or four times. "Fuck!"

Sedotal leaned back against the seat and closed his eyes. Sage checked his arm then stared at Grier. "This shit never happened when you made the runs with us." At first, he spoke as if he believed Grier was the reason no one dared try to hit a Demon job. Then, he spoke softer. "Where were you tonight?"

Sage knew Grier had only come home because Fiona threatened him. How he'd found out, Grier had no real idea, but he knew. But he hadn't questioned Grier's loyalty to Fiona and the Demons until right now. And it pissed Grier off.

"You think I did this?" Oh wow. It hadn't occurred to him that Sage would question Grier. Of course, he'd questioned Sage, so it was… fair.

Sage shrugged—not in a confused kind of way, but in the he-didn't-believe-a-fucking-word-Grier-said kind of way. "It's just funny that the one night you have mysterious stuff to do, we get hijacked and set on fire. Doesn't seem to be much of a coincidence."

Since Sage was Grier's only real friend since Kye was in Belize, Grier didn't want to kick his ass, but if Sage went any further down that thorny little path, what choice would he have? "Watch it, man."

"No big deal. Just tell me where you were. It's all cleared up then." His tone, matter-of-fact, made his words sound far less important than Grier found them.

Grier glanced at Sedotal in the mirror. He might have been out of it, or he might have been pretending. Grier couldn't tell. Neither did he want to tell Sage what he'd been up to. Without proof against them, Grier would look like an asshole for not believing in Sage. It wouldn't matter so much about Sedotal since everyone already knew Grier hated him, but he couldn't blame one without the other. Not yet. Plus, no point in tipping them off so that they were more careful next time.

"Out." He cleared his throat. "With Fiona."

"With Fiona?"

"Yeah." Easy lie. And no way Sage would question her about it. "We're talking a little." And to make sure, he added, "Fucking a lot."

Sage nodded and smiled. "That's great, man." He glanced back. Grier could hardly see the truck anymore or the orange and red glow above it, but a fire truck blew past, lights spinning, siren blaring.

He swore again. Harder. Loud enough Sedotal sat straight again. "What?!" He blinked a couple of times and looked around.

Grier had a lot to work out. A line across the road could have killed them. Probably would have if it was done right. Of course, the competency of the killers wasn't something he could count on. He could check the bikes though. The damage would tell the story. Still, Grier knew Sage, knew he loved that bike and wouldn't risk a scratch just to throw Grier off his scent, and it definitely looked like he'd come off his bike, laid it down. Besides, Sage was a "collector" at the club. If he wanted to steal, there were much easier ways to do it than this.

Sedotal, on the other hand, looked more like he'd taken a blow to the head. Wouldn't have been a picnic for him if it was faked, but if he'd been put down, he should've been a little more messed up than a single gash in his forehead.

And no matter what, the merchandise in the truck was gone. Whatever could be salvaged would be taken into evidence—no way the Demons could claim it—the rest would be tossed after the crime guys got finished. And there would be crime guys since the driver had been in the truck. Poor bastard.

And while the truck was unregistered with stolen plates, he didn't know if the driver had left any paperwork that would somehow survive the fire and lead the cops to the clubhouse door. Or if fingerprints would or could be lifted off the door or the boxes inside or… anywhere else. For now, he'd have to hope not.

More than any of that, though, he had to figure out how this happened. Someone had lit the fire. Someone who wanted to pick up all the lost Demon business. Or someone with a grudge. Not like the Demons made friends easy. But they controlled a lot of the "free enter-prise" in and around Pine Hill. Also could've been someone or a group of someones looking to edge out the Demons. Fuck. Could've been anyone. Even the cops.

He dialed the clubhouse as he turned onto the turn-pike. He needed to get Sage to Jez so she could clean him up. Sedotal, too. It wouldn't do for the fucker to die in the backseat of the rental. He hadn't gotten the insurance.

No answer. He called Hamilton direct. "Yeah?"

"Get the trailer. Sage and Sedotal laid their bikes down off the 93 by Medford. We need to get those bikes back to the club." He didn't want to say more now. He'd talk to Hamilton when he got a moment alone. "Jez still around?"

"Nah. She left a couple of hours ago for dinner with Fiona." Grier shot a sideways glance at Sage hoping he couldn't hear Hamilton's deep voice.

Grier switched the phone to his opposite ear. He waited a second to be sure then said, "Call her back. We need her. They're both hurt."

"How bad?" Hamilton wasn't completely healed, but thank God, he sounded better than he had even a week ago.

"Not sure. Can't take them to the hospital though." There would have to be protruding bones and a lot more blood for a hospital visit.

"Gotcha." Hamilton hung up, and Grier glanced again at Sage. He stared out the window, still holding his arm.

"You hurt anywhere else?" Nothing he could do, but he needed to see how Sage answered.

"No." But he didn't look at Grier, and it didn't take a genius to know that was bad.

16

Fiona stared at the little blue plus sign as she held the phone with her shoulder. She couldn't concentrate on everything Sage had said. She made him repeat it again. "He lied. He said… God Fiona, he said he was with you."

"With me?" He'd used her as his alibi? After ignoring her for a month, accusing her of screwing Tyler Sedotal, and keeping his own nasty little set of secrets.

"Yeah, but I knew you and Jez were going out to dinner. She told me it was girls' night." He sighed. "I wanted it to be anybody but him." Sadness made his voice quiet.

Fiona knew, had known, Grier hadn't wanted to come back from Belize. Knew he didn't want to be married to her—he'd certainly proved that time after time. But she never would have thought, or even considered he would go this far—trying to ruin the club—to get out.

She needed to get off the phone. Didn't even say goodbye—couldn't—before she hung up and sank to the floor next to her bed.

And she'd been dumb enough to get pregnant. Not that she couldn't raise a baby on her own, but she would have to tell that baby that its father…

Oh, God. Hamilton would kill him. And if he didn't, the others would. Grier was a dead man walking. A picture of him flashed through her mind. Standing in her shower, singing some horrible eighties tune while he washed his hair oblivious to Fiona watching from the doorway.

Tears slipped down her cheeks, and she swiped at them for a while then gave up. They came faster than she could flick them away. She would have sold the house for a drink, but she couldn't. Her baby would have every chance she could give it.

Suffering through this without alcohol wouldn't kill her. Her broken heart might, though.

No. She didn't care about Grier. He'd proved he wasn't worthy of being cared about.

She didn't care who knocked at the door—persistently. Probably Hamilton. Sage would have told him by now that Grier was the rat, the traitor, the son of a bitch who was trying to bankrupt the club. And while he knew what had to be done, he wouldn't do it without her say-so. Not because Grier was her husband, but because she was the president, the boss, the go-to girl for all club decisions.

Tomorrow, she would call for a vote. Tonight, she earned the right to cry out her feelings.

She looked again at the pregnancy test in her hand. Threw it across the room and watched it break apart into five or six pieces of jagged plastic.

When the front door opened and closed, she dried her face with her palms and stood. Okay. Crying could wait. She walked into the hallway and slammed into Grier's chest.

He looked down at her, holding her shoulders to keep her steady. She wiggled free and stepped back.

"Have you been crying?"

She cleared her throat and hoped she could sound as angry as she felt. Or at least as sarcastic. "Yes, Grier. I cry myself to sleep every night you're not here."

He didn't grin. Didn't come back with some sexy answer that would make her toes curl inside her shoes. He stood still, not blinking. Maybe not even breathing. "Fiona, we have to talk."

He turned and walked downstairs. She took a second to expel the breath she'd been holding before following him down. With his back to her, so she didn't have to look into his lying eyes, she could have imagined he was there for her, had come to tell her he wanted their marriage to work. But her mind told her heart to shut the hell up. He didn't want to be with her. Wouldn't want their kid. Wouldn't be any better of a father than he'd been husband.

But she needed to hear what he had to say, decide how she would handle it. Letting Hamilton have him would kill her. "What do you want?"

He turned and raked his fingers through his hair. It hung free around his face and fell back as soon as he moved his hands. "Sit down."

"It's my house, Grier. I'll decide if I sit or stand." She wouldn't let him tower over her while he talked. "What do you want?" She couldn't find a better question.

"The shipments."

Oh, God. Was he here to confess?

"What about them?"

He sat on the coffee table, leaned with his elbows on his knees, and folded his hands in front of him. "It's an inside job, and I should've told you."

Yeah. Quite the understatement there. "Why didn't you?"

"I wasn't sure." He hung his head. "I'm still not."

God, she hated him. Everything about him. Except she didn't. She only hoped that if she told herself she did often enough, eventually, she'd believe it. "Then why are you here?"

A little part of her wanted him to tell her he'd come for her. A very little part. The third eyelash from the left on her right eye. That part of her hoped…

"Because Sage is going to call you and tell you I lied to him." His voice cracked and Fiona looked up. "And you're going to believe him because I've been a shit. An asshole, even."

She nodded. "Yeah." He'd been worse than that, but she remained silent.

"And I'm so sorry, Fi." He stood, and she backed up a step. Grier nodded and closed his eyes. "He already called."

"You lied about where you were tonight."

"That doesn't mean I would do this. I would never hurt you or this club."

Oh, that was rich. The most ridiculous lie he'd told yet. She cocked an eyebrow. "Seriously? That's what you're going with?" Fire burned in her blood. "You wouldn't hurt me? Well, let's see if that's true, shall we?" Dear Lord, there were so many ways to prove that a lie, she didn't even know where to start. "You have done nothing but hurt me since you've been back. You don't come home. You fuck me senseless then walk out and accuse me of screwing Tyler Sedotal." Yeah. That one hurt. "My dad trusted you even though you ran out on us, all of us, for your little friend and his… woman." She shook her head, hoping for the strength to make it through kicking his ass out of her house. "Everything you've said and everything you've done since you came back from your little island paradise has been a lie."

"Fiona." The pain in his voice almost undid her will. And when he reached for her, she curled her fingers into a fist. She would not touch him. No sir.

"Don't. Please. Don't."

"You have to listen to me. Please." Softer, he said again, "Please."

She shrugged as if her heart hadn't shattered, as if she had more than a few minutes before she'd be a sobbing mess worthy of a telethon in her benefit. And because her legs wouldn't support her anymore, she moved to the sofa and sat. "Is this gonna be a dramatic performance? Should I get a popcorn and soda?"

He sighed and sat on the table again in front of her. "I lied about tonight because I was waiting to tail the truck." He looked down. "I wanted to follow Sage and Sedotal."

"Why?" It didn't take a genius to turn the tables and throw his friends under that runaway bus.

"Because. Every time, one or both of them knew the details of every stolen shipment. The routes that were taken, even when you switched up and used decoy trucks. Decoy trucks that no one ever bothered."

"That doesn't prove anything." She knew, Grier knew, and Hamilton knew, too.

"No. It doesn't. But on every shipment over the last two weeks, I went on the runs. Put a tracker in each truck we escorted back. No hits. I don't know if Sedotal knew about them, but I know Sage knew." He shook his head. "But they didn't know I put one in today's truck. I went to our distributor early today and had him put the tracker in one of the boxes today before Sage and Sedotal got there."

"Trackers?" His big secret. And a good idea, she had to admit.

His leg kicked out straight as he fumbled in his pocket. He pulled a little piece of electronic equipment and held it up for her. "Yes. One of these."

Fiona took it. Stared at it as if she had any idea how the damned thing worked. A piece of plastic so tiny she could hold it in her palm and no one would know she had it certainly couldn't be powerful enough to catch their bastard thief. Of course, it could be something else. Something like a hearing aid maybe or a new-fangled, ultra-small phone charger. She didn't know enough about technology to fill a pea pod. "Some CIA shit? You a NARC now, too?"

"No. An electronics store and an app on my phone." He sighed. "Look, Fi. I know I hurt you." He closed his eyes. "And I know I've been a bad husband. But you know me. I'm not a thief, and I gave my word to Max. I promised him I would protect you and this club. I might not be a good man, but I'm true to my word and you know it." His eyes, darker green with emotion, searched hers.

In spite of everything, she wanted to believe him. But there was too much circumstantial shit against him. Not the least of which was how he'd treated her. Used her. Knocked her up and left her. Although in his defense, he disappeared before he ever knew he knocked her up.

She tossed the little receiver or transponder or tracker or whatever it was back to him. "What do you want me to say, Grier?" She'd thought of the baby, and that was her mistake. She needed to get this over with.

"I want you to say you believe me and that you know I wouldn't do this. And that you trust me."

She would have laughed had he not been so serious. "You know what I know about you, Grier? I know that you can fuck like a god. And you can run like a Jamaican Olympian. But I don't believe you. I don't know you. And I don't trust you." She ignored the wounded puppy look in his eyes.

"I'm innocent and you're going to let them kill me."

Another thing she would have to explain to her baby. She swallowed a batch of tears back. "They won't vote until tomorrow. You can leave tonight. Get a flight back to Belize with Kye. We'll be fine." And as if she had no control, or maybe her subconscious wanted him to guess, she laid a hand over her stomach.

"We?" He swallowed hard as a flicker of fear danced in his eyes.

Not how she wanted to tell him. And not a reason she would let him use to stay and die. "The club. Me and the club equals *we*." She dropped her hand and ran it along the fabric of the cushion next to her. She found the motion soothing. Plus, it dried her sweaty palm.

"You're…" He glanced at her stomach again, stared for a second as if trying to see through her skin to what she might be—okay, was absolutely— hiding inside. "Wanting me to go? You'll lose everything."

If the club killed him, she lost everything, too. "Maybe. But you'll still be alive." And no matter what else happened, that mattered to her.

Grier watched Fiona. Her eyelids fluttered. She cared. "Fi, you can save me, you know. You just have to believe in me."

"You want me to lie for you?" Disbelief either in him or for what he was asking her to do lowered her voice to a whisper.

It stung, but he deserved it. "Show them the tracker. Sage will verify that much at least."

"Grier."

He could have charmed her, used the tone of voice he knew she loved, the one that made her purr. But he wanted her on his side, not counseling him to run again. Not when she was… maybe… probably… pregnant. And he couldn't really blame her for not telling him. Not when she thought he was the one selling out the club.

God. He'd made so many mistakes. Ruined his chance with Fiona. But he couldn't run again. Especially if she was pregnant. "Fiona. Do you believe I would've lied to Max? That I would betray you all? That I would hurt *you* like this?"

"It doesn't matter what I think." She blinked a few times, quickly, the way she'd done just before she'd cried when she was younger. Oh, God. He didn't want to see her cry. No way he could take it right now without falling apart in front of her. And he didn't want that either.

"It matters to me." He wanted—needed—her to believe in him.

But he'd stay anyway. Even if they wanted to kill him. He wouldn't make it easy for them, but he wouldn't be flying to Belize either. Dying was one thing. Running out on his family was another. And like it or not, Fiona and the baby were his family.

She chewed the corner of her lip then soothed the spot with her tongue. "If I tell them I knew about the transmitter trackers"—she waved a hand as if she had the name close enough—"and you turn out to be the guy screwing the club over... I'll kill you myself if I have to fly to Belize and shoot you on a beach."

He believed her, and her agreement said she believed him. That was enough for now. About the club anyway.

But he couldn't leave yet. Not until he knew if she was carrying his baby. He gazed at her. Stared, really. Hard enough she fidgeted—and fuck if he didn't find that as attractive and elegant as everything else she did.

He only needed to ask the question. She wouldn't lie. Or maybe she would. Maybe she would find lying to him easier than lying for him.

"I'm pregnant." She swiped her hands against her sofa—one on the armrest, the other on the cushion next to her. The fabric changed from light to dark and back with each brush of her fingers. "And I know you believe I screwed Tyler, but I didn't. The baby's yours."

He nodded. "I know." He swallowed hard, heart in his gut.

"You do?" Her eyebrows squished toward the center of her face. "I thought you…"

"No. I was being stupid." He glanced at her stomach. A baby. *His* baby. No way he could run. Kye had been right. "You… I guess you got what you wanted, huh?"

She watched him from narrow eyes. Her lips formed a tight line. "Oh, yeah. Exactly what I wanted." She shrugged. "Husband who'd rather sleep in the back of cars than with me. Who all my best friends think is a traitor. Again. Who only married me because my dad had a gun to his head. And now a baby for him to ignore, too. Isn't that every girl's dream?"

He could stand her sarcasm. Even the absolute incorrectness of every damned thing she'd just said, but the tears in her eyes undid any resolve he had left. His plan to leave left without him. "Fiona…" He moved to sit beside her and draw her against him, almost sighed when she didn't shove him off the couch. "I just want to say, for the record, that there isn't any place I'd rather sleep than with you."

"It's these damned hormones." She sniffled and pulled away to dry her eyes. "I haven't cried this much since…" She glanced up, pointed a slow smile at him, and ran her hand down his arm. "Since that day you left me at the mall."

"You cried?" God, if she knew what it had taken for him to walk away, to not tear that sexy little get-up off of her, she would have been prancing around with pride, not crying.

"I was so humiliated. I told my friend Jackie all about this guy I was going to give my virginity to. I mean, I had such a crush on you and being twenty years old and a virgin in a place where virginity isn't quite the honor it is in church was horrible." She shook her head. "Then I had to go crying back to her how that guy didn't want me."

He chuckled and pulled her close again. "Oh, God,

Fiona. If you only knew how much I wanted you." He stroked her arm with his thumb. "I didn't walk right for a week."

"You walked out on me well enough." She let her hand drop to his lap. "I have a distinct memory of watching you slam open the dressing room door and stomp through the lingerie store so quickly you made a breeze inside."

It was easy to smile about it now, when it was the lightest of the heavy things they needed to discuss. "I'm sorry. If I had known how important to you it was…"

"You're the one that took me for the wax and spray tan. Who watched me buy an ounce of perfume for four-hundred-dollars because of the pheromones."

And she hadn't needed any of it. "If it wasn't for Max, I would have…"

He didn't finish because the hand she'd dropped onto his thigh was no longer inactive or stationary. It brushed against his zipper, and his cock came to life. With one simple touch from Fiona, it threatened to burst through his zipper.

"Max isn't here now." Her voice came on a breathy sigh as she flicked the button of pants open. And God help him, he yelped. "And even if he was, he sanctioned this whole thing. You. Me. A baby."

They needed to talk about the baby, needed to figure out what to do about missing shipments and whether or not the Screaming Demons would be holding a bonfire tomorrow night to celebrate his death. But damned if he could think of one reasonable thing to say about any of it. And any thought faded when she slid off the sofa then knelt in front of him.

She smiled and wrapped her fingers around his dick, stroking lightly at first. "You know, I wanted to be the one who made all the rules for us. In bed and out. But…" She slid her tongue from the base of his cock to the tip and when her tongue swirled around the head, he almost lost it. This woman knew how to shred all of his control. She looked up at him. "Turns out, I like when you tell me what to do. When you watch me. When you spank me for breaking a rule." She lowered her head again. "But tonight, I'm the one who'll be giving all the orders, who is going to tell you what to do."

"Yeah?"

"The first time anyway. After that… we'll see."

His mouth went dry and his pulse pounded in his ears. "As you wish."

She took him into her mouth this time, and when he closed his eyes, she stopped and lifted her head. "Watch me."

He opened his eyes, watched her for a second before his eyelids fluttered closed, and she stopped again. "Grier, you're not listening."

This woman and her magical mouth. "I can't help it. It's so… incredible."

She stood to straddle his lap then climbed off. "Take your pants off." His dick, still in her hand, twitched. When he stood, she stood with him. "And do it sexy."

This might have been payback for when he'd made her get dressed just to strip for him. But he didn't care. Something about that predatory look in her eyes made this so hot.

And she'd danced on him, gyrated until he couldn't stop touching himself until she bent over in front of him. Oh yeah. He would return that favor.

He pulled out his phone, hit an icon and said, "Play Fiona's dance mix." A slow steady pulse of music pumped out the speaker and he stroked his cock in time to the beat while she watched, eyes glowing, breath a little faster.

When he moved closer and thrust his hips forward, she reached for him, and he moved back. She lowered her hand and sat on the edge of the coffee table. The music picked up tempo and he swirled his hips. Now his cock had her full attention, and he had to stop touching himself when she slipped her tongue across her lower lip.

He took her hands and guided them under his shirt. And in a fair is fair kind of move, she tweaked his nipples so that he gasped.

"You like that?" She did it again, then pulled him closer and pushed his shirt up enough she could take his nipple into her mouth, pinch it between her teeth.

Oh, fuck. If he didn't slow this down, he was going to come. He pulled away, his lungs unsteady and possibly confused about how they were supposed to work.

She ran her hand over her pussy, and his world spun. Aside from being buried deep inside her, tasting her while she screamed his name, and watching her face when she came, there was nothing he liked more than when she pleased herself. He moved in again, legs apart so she fit between, and his cock was at her eye level. A bead of cum glistened on the top and when she tongued it away, he moaned.

She stood and pressed her body into his, shoved the shirt up, and he lifted his arms so she could get it out of the way. When she tossed it over her shoulder, she went for his pants.

"Thought you wanted me to dance for you."

"Changed my mind, Magic Mike. I want you to fuck me. Right here. Right now." Sultry but demanding, she pushed him onto the sofa, shed her own pants and straddled his lap.

A day that started with so little promise ended with Grier and Fiona wrapped together, basking in the afterglow.

17

Fiona sat at the head of the table. They'd had a couple of small meetings since she'd taken her father's place, but never one where the entire room was full, with the exception of Grier's seat at her right hand which remained empty. He hadn't come to tell his own story.

Tyler Sedotal—not a Screaming Demon, just a security guard—stood at the door. Sage was to her left a few chairs down, Hamilton next to her. Frank, Nate, and Owen all sat in chairs and some of the other guys who would normally be seated stood and others filled their spots. It didn't matter. Everyone in this room with the exception of Hamilton, Fiona and normally Grier, were equals. And of course, Sedotal.

She'd already shown them the tracking device, told them she and Grier had made the plan together. Now it was a matter of hashing it out among themselves as to whether or not they trusted not just Grier, but her word as well. This was as much her moment of truth as his. But damned if she would let them see her waver or falter. She banged the small gavel against a block of varnished and stained wood. The table in her spot was scarred because her father liked the crash and echo when he hit the table. Fiona liked the table better.

Sage nodded along with Hamilton who defended Grier. "He came back knowing we all hated him and would have killed him. But all that time he was away, he was protecting our assets, not selling us out." He shook his head. "I know you don't all know him that well, and Max, may he rest in peace, was from a different era when we killed first and asked questions later, but he trusted Grier, let him marry Max's most prized possession. And if Max was here now to listen to you all doubting Fiona's word, he would take out his gun and shoot every one of you."

Fiona wanted to smile, but it wasn't the time. She hadn't asked Hamilton to defend her or Grier. But his loyalty to Max knew no bounds. And normally, where Hamilton led, others followed. Maybe out of fear, or maybe because he never led them astray.

But Sedotal stepped forward. "He's her husband. Of course, she's going to say he's innocent."

"You're the hired help, not a Demon."

And thank you, Nate.

"What's he even doing here?" Frank mumbled the words toward Fiona, but she stared at Sedotal.

"Golden boy couldn't protect her so she hired me. Or maybe she hired me so her boyfriend"—he rolled his eyes—"husband could practice his pathetic fighting skills." He pushed through a crowd of Demons to brace both hands on the table next to Fiona. "He's not the guy you think he is. Why don't you ask him who else he's doing his little strip dances for? Ask him where else he's been putting his dick after he arranges to fuck over the club."

What? She kept her face impassive, but her heart kicked into gear. She'd never asked Grier if he'd been with anyone else. Never even considered it. But he hadn't been home. And guys like him—sensual, flirty, beautiful—didn't spend their nights alone. And with Hell Kats aplenty wandering around, he would've had his pick. She would have loved to give him the benefit of the doubt. It would have soothed her even, but their history, including the most recent months, didn't dip the needle in his favor.

She smiled at Sedotal because killing him right then wouldn't have done anything to help her position now that he'd planted seeds of doubt in both the club and her own mind. "This is club business. And you're not part of the club. Maybe you should wait outside."

"Let me kill him for you. He's a traitor and a cheater and a liar. You deserve better."

"He's a Screaming Demon and you're not. Get out."

Hamilton stood, and Tyler lifted both hands in surrender. And while he glared as if he wanted to punch Hamilton, he turned and walked to the door.

She'd had enough for today. It was time to vote.

FIONA SAT on the examination table wrapped in her paper gown with a second paper "blanket" thrown over her legs. The stirrups stared ominously. She hadn't known it would be this kind of appointment or she wouldn't have invited Grier.

The shade of his skin turned greener and greener with every word he read from a pamphlet he'd plucked from a rack on the wall. He held it toward Fiona. "That's what's going to happen to your…" He pointed as if he hadn't deigned to say the word *pussy* or even the more clinical *vagina.*

The picture showed the stages of delivery. "Speaking of what's going to happen to my… area, I was just wondering…" Wondering, hell. She hadn't been able to think of anything else since Sedotal made his accusation. "Should I be getting an STD check?" He stared at her. "I mean, um, you've been gone… and I just don't… I haven't, but I didn't know if you…"

He stood and took her hand. "I've been with four women in my life. Kelly Pruitt when I was fifteen. A Hell Kat I was faithful to until she left." Fiona remembered her. Knew how hurt he'd been when Autumn—okay, they could just call it *left*. "An island girl when I was away. And you." He squeezed her hand. "And as long as you're my wife, there will only be you and no one else, no matter if I live with you or not."

When the doctor knocked and pushed the door open, Grier moved back to his chair, and if Fiona's heart could smile, it had to be smiling. No words had ever made her happier.

* * *

SHE SIPPED her water and watched as Grier attacked his hamburger. "Just admit it. You saw our kid on that screen and you cried. It's okay. I liked it."

"If I cried, which I didn't, it would only be because I couldn't see the kid on the screen. It all looked like black and white blobs to me."

Oh, he could say what he wanted—and he'd tried everything from dust in his eye to jealousy over the size of the ultrasound wand—but when he saw their kid even in its black and white blob form, he'd teared up. Like a real father.

He lifted his burger again, then sat it back down. "And maybe—*if* I cried—it was because my wife seemed so hopeful when she asked if she had to back off from having sex so it wouldn't hurt the baby."

She grinned. "I was hopeful. Hopeful he'd say we could have all the sex we wanted." And thank God he had, because these days, she wanted a lot.

A woman at the next table widened her eyes, and Fiona, whose moods shifted like a summer wind, shot her a scowl. "What? Mind your business. Unless I drag him onto this table and rip his clothes off in front of you"—an idea she could probably get behind—"what we do or talk about over here is none of your business."

"Fi." Grier gave her hand a squeeze. "Eat, babe. I think you're hangry."

The woman picked up her plate and glass and moved to a booth across the room. "She was nosy." After a minute, Fiona rolled her eyes. Maybe she had been talking louder than necessary. "Fine." But instead of getting up to apologize, she slipped off her shoes and laid her foot on the chair between his legs and rubbed it over his dick.

"What are you doing?" He had a sexy, playful tone that matched the sideways glance and glint in his eyes.

"Stretching. Thinking about throwing you on this table and tearing your clothes off."

Grier waved for the waitress. "Could we get the check?"

Fiona threw her head back and laughed, but if he thought she was kidding, he was in for a long, surprising afternoon.

* * *

GRIER WATCHED FIONA SLEEP. One of his new favorite things to do. Along with holding her. Touching her. Lying beside her. Even talking to her about anything.

He might have come back to Pine Hill under duress, even married her because he was forced, but the tingling in his chest when he looked at her, the weak knees, the way every thought centered around her and them as a couple, that was all him. Out of his control, but all him.

And it scared the shit out of him. He had no idea how to be a husband. Or a father. He knew violence and death. Not a legacy he wanted to pass onto his kid.

Leaving would be the right thing to do, the best thing for Fiona and the baby. But the selfish bastard in him wanted her, the kid, the family he'd never had.

He eased his arm from beneath her and took his phone into the bathroom. He found Kye's number and waited while it rang.

Kye skipped a hello. "Mrs. Strong, it's three in the morning. Have you no respect for time zones?"

"It's three a.m. here, too, dumb ass." And not at all why he'd called.

"Okay. Whatever. What's up?"

"Fiona's pregnant." Kye would have words of wisdom. He'd read every book ever written practically.

"Shit."

But first they had to get the issue straight. "I'm kind of okay with it."

"Really?" Was it really such a strange idea that he would be happy about being a father?

"Yeah." He smiled. The truth came to him the moment he'd said it. More than okay with it. "Except I don't know much about kids or changing diapers or… teaching them… stuff." He sounded like a whiny teenager.

Kye chuckled. "Look, your job is basically getting the kid's name tattooed on your arm and staying out of Fiona's way. Women have these God-given instincts about kids. She'll know what to do."

But the banging on the bathroom door along with the heavy breathing as she called out to him contradicted Kye with volume. "I gotta go."

He set the phone down and let her in. Before he had the door open more than a crack, she shoved it out of her way and threw herself against him, arms around his waist and head buried in his chest. Her tears ran down her face and his body. "I had the worst dream."

"Want to tell me about it?" Good husbands asked questions like that. Plus, he really did want to help her.

"I dreamt I lost the baby."

His arms came around her, squeezed. "We'll make sure you get the best medical care out there. Even if we have to fly to Europe or... California." How the hell would he know where good medical care existed? He'd probably seen a doctor twice in his adult life, once for a gunshot wound and once for a broken leg.

"Not miscarried. Lost. Misplaced. Forgot where I put him." She shook her head and sniffled. "I had him with me when I went shopping." And as if he had any control over her dreams, she looked up and scowled at him. "For your birthday present."

"Sorry?"

"I sat him down to get my wallet out of this ridiculous bubble gum pink purse. Then I just walked out without him. I got home and had to go back, but I couldn't remember which store I was in. Then I kept going in circles, and I couldn't find him. I was calling out for him, you know, like a baby could answer. 'Kermit! Kermit!'"

Grier shook his head. "We are *not* naming our kid Kermit." Dear God, no. If she had any idea how he'd suffered with that name as a kid, she would never have suggested it.

She blew out a breath through her clenched teeth. "Not the point. Then when I woke up and you were gone, I thought I lost you, too."

"I'm not going anywhere, and you won't misplace our kid." Of course, he couldn't guarantee that. The kid part. But no damned way would she lose him. "We'll get a leash or something."

"We can't put our baby on a leash." She leaned back to look at him. "When's your birthday?"

"April." She cocked her head and pulled her lips into a twisted pout. "The ninth."

"Maybe we should change it. Or celebrate it at a different time."

He would if she asked. He didn't really care about his birthday anyway. Growing up, it had just been another day that came and went, reinforcing that he had no one to care for. "Okay." Curiosity, though. "But why?"

"So my dream doesn't come true." He didn't tell her that it wasn't the date that mattered, or the shopping, but she rolled her eyes and stalked back to the bed, flung the covers back, and flopped under, keeping her back to Grier's side of the bed.

He watched, morbid fascination coupling with extreme confusion.

"Fi? Are you okay?"

"I'm fine." She sat up and punched her pillow a couple of times before slamming her head back down.

And because he knew nothing about pregnancy hormones other than that they existed, he stayed in the bathroom. "Did you want me to… sleep in here?" He dared not suggest the couch.

She sat up and her eyes brimmed with tears, almost like she'd turned on a faucet. "Oh, no!" Her wail rang through the quiet in the room and spurred Grier into action.

He slipped under the blanket and pulled her back against his chest as she sobbed into her pillow. "Shh. It's okay. I just didn't want to bother you. I *want* to sleep here. With you. Every night."

It took a second before she turned to look up at him. He dried her eyes with his thumb then kissed the end of her nose. "Is that okay?"

"More than okay."

And while it was the truth, the idea of leaving her for her own good and the good of their child lurked in a quiet corner of his mind.

18

No one told her being pregnant would make her lose her damned mind. Or turn her into a blubbering mass of tears and snot. Also, no one mentioned fingers that looked like smoke sausage links, disappearing ankles, sore boobs, acne, or exactly how tired she'd be.

All she'd ever heard about was how women glowed when they were carrying their babies. If Fiona glowed, it could only be because she had to pee. Every minute of every day. And the mood swings… oh, God, the mood swings. One minute she wanted Grier more than she wanted to take her next breath. The next, she couldn't stand any more questions—*how're you feeling, can I get you anything, want me to rub your feet*—and hated the sight of him. She despised his good mood. And loved it.

He'd been coming home, but even that would change if she didn't figure out how to work this out.

"What do I do?"

Jez sat across from her, listening as Fiona poured out the whole sordid thing. "He bought a crib?" Fiona glared at her. Jez was going to come down on Grier's side—apparently, they had sides now—and she'd been Fiona's friend first, owed her loyalty to Fiona. Jez scowled. "That bastard."

"I just thought it was something we'd do together, you know? And he comes home with one then spent three hours—like there were no directions included in the box or something—putting it together. And it's beautiful." Her voice went soft. "It's round and has a canopy that drapes over it." But dammit, it would only work for a little girl. No boy of hers would sleep in such a feminine baby bed. She softened. Of course he would because his father cared enough to go out and spend nine hundred dollars on a bed for him. And if he grew up feminine, she would be absolutely fine with it.

Jez put a hand over her mouth. "Girl, you should see your face. One minute you're pouty and petulant, the next happy as a clam in the sand."

"Do I need to go to the doctor? Is this a normal thing?" She lowered her voice. "I don't want to drive him away."

Jez laughed. "You know what? First, he helped get

you this way. He'll be fine. And if not, you don't want him anyway."

Oh, but she did want him. Forever. Not that she had the courage to tell him. Or would likely ever have the courage to tell him.

"Second." Jez stared at Fiona hard. "I think you love that boy."

Love? No. Love meant missing him when they were apart. Looking forward to seeing him. Wanting to spend every minute together in his arms. Dying to hear anything and everything he had to say. Needing to… Oh, hell.

She swallowed hard. She didn't want to blurt her feelings out for the whole restaurant to hear. "No."

Jez patted her hand. "Your daddy would be so proud. It's all he ever wanted for you."

And had she not been so intent on denying her feelings, she would have teared up again at the mention of her father, but now she stared at Jez, wondering if Grier had somehow read her the way Jez had.

"I don't love Grier." That lie burned in her throat, leaving her with no choice but to argue it into truth.

"Okay." Jez's disbelief turned her voice into one of those cartoon character sounds.

"I'm serious. I like being with him fine, but I could live without him." Oh yeah. She'd have to work on making that one convincing, too. "I mean… I would miss him, of course, but…" She couldn't imagine not having him near enough to touch. She'd even tried to get out of dinner tonight so she could stay with him. "Jez, I'm screwed."

Jez laughed. "No, baby. You are head over heels. And it's beautiful. And exciting. An adventure the two of you can take together."

"What if he doesn't…?"

"He does."

"What if he…?"

Jez laughed. "He bought you the baby bed of your dreams. He doesn't even look at the Wall Kats or the Hell Kats. And baby, they're doing a lot of looking at him."

The vein in her temple throbbed. "Who is?"

"He's good-looking. Women notice. Don't worry. I put out the word that he's off-limits."

"Who. Is. Looking. At. My. Husband?"

Jez shook her head. "You don't know her."

"Lisa? Maggie? Jez, I don't want to have to ask again." And she hadn't meant it to sound like a threat. She really didn't want to ask again.

"Autumn."

Fiona slammed her hand on the table. What the fuck was she doing back? Fiona had made Max send her away a long time ago. She would've thought Autumn would have gotten the message back then.

"Look, Fi, she rode in with Kale. He didn't know, and she didn't know. I told her. And now she knows." Jez chased her out of the restaurant as she lifted her arm to wave down a cab. "Fiona!"

"I'm not going to kill her. I'm just going to make very clear that Grier is spoken for, and if she tries anything, I'll put her right back on the wall she slithered off of." Okay. There were perks to being the chick in charge.

Fiona climbed in the cab and Jez slid in beside her. "What about your car?"

Jez had driven them to the restaurant. "I'll get it tomorrow. I can't have you running off all hormonal and jealous. With the way you've been treating Grier, he might be more inclined to leave you in jail than bail you out. So I need to make sure you don't do anything stupid."

Fiona flipped her hair over her shoulder. "Fine, but if I have to punch her in the throat, just know it isn't going to have one damned thing to do with my hormones." Jez pulled out her phone and shot off a short, fast text. Fiona scowled. "Did you warn her?"

"Warned Grier." She held up her phone. The screen read, *Fiona warpath. Meet at club.*

"Succinct."

"Thanks. I've been working on my text skills."

Fiona fumed all the way across town, on the turnpike, through the neighborhood where she'd played as a child. Finally, he pulled into the parking lot. Fiona threw some cash over the seat and swung her legs out of the car. She strolled past Grier's bike and into the bar. No Autumn. No Grier. Her blood boiled.

He'd just spent days telling her how he wouldn't hurt her. Wouldn't leave. Wouldn't… she couldn't even remember all the promises he'd made. She stomped through a huddle of Demons to the bar. Lisa put a beer in front of her—they hadn't told anyone but Jez, Hamilton and Sage about the baby. "Where's Autumn?"

Angry Fiona never bothered with niceties like greetings. "Back room with…"

Fiona didn't stick around to hear his name. She stalked to the hallway that led to the rooms with beds and half-naked chicks hanging on the walls. As she opened the first room—empty except for the poster— she made a mental note to tear those damned things down as she slammed that one and moved to the next. It took three before she heard a high-pitched female squeal. She shoved in and stopped. Autumn, naked and straddling Hamilton, covered herself as she scampered off the bed.

"What the hell, Fi?"

"Uh, carry on." Her skin had to be the color of a Sox uniform for all the burning just underneath. She backed out of the room and sauntered back to the bar where

Grier stood leaning against the bar, her beer in his hand and his cocky smile in place.

"I think we'll talk about this at home." But he wrapped his arms around her. Even though she'd, once again, distrusted him.

She nodded. At least he was coming home.

His breath warmed her ear as he pulled her against him and lowered his head to whisper, "Somebody might need a spanking."

And again with the hormones, she pulled her lower lip between her teeth. "We could take care of that here." Her panties went damp just thinking about it.

"No. Here's what I want you to do." He kissed her neck just below her earlobe. "I want you to go home, get undressed, and wait for me."

"How long will you be?" She was already hot and panting.

"Long enough for you to send me a video of you touching yourself."

A video? That was a lot of trust to give someone. "Grier."

He smiled softly and leaned his forehead against hers. "It's okay, babe. And don't worry. I'll still give you your spanking later." His voice had that sexy growl quality she'd come to—dare she think it?—love.

And love meant trust. She kissed him hard and fast. "Keep your phone close, babe."

She turned and went out the door. Trust truly was a many splendored thing. And so was the night she planned to have with her husband.

* * *

GRIER RACED his bike toward home, Sage riding next to him. Fiona had indeed sent a video, but while she might have done as he asked, she'd hit a button wrong or forgot she hadn't turned it on. The video she'd sent started when Tyler Sedotal walked into her house.

What are you doing here?

Grier couldn't see, but he'd certainly heard Sedotal's drunken answer. *I came to show you how a real man treats his woman.*

Still no picture, but Grier heard glass shatter. Her voice came in a shriek. *Get away from me.* She kept a gun in the hallway closet, and Grier hoped she was making her way toward it.

You walk around like you're so tough. But I've watched you letting that piece of shit tell you what to do. Do you really like it when he tells you to suck his dick or is that an act? Because if it's an act, you're wasting your time here. You should be in Hollywood.

Watched? That word stuck with Grier. Had that fucker been in the house again? Watching them when they thought they were alone? It didn't matter. Grier was going to kill him. Tyler Sedotal would never see another thing again.

Fuck you. But her voice trembled. Grier should never have sent her home alone. His fault. All his fucking fault.

Oh, you're going to. Just like you do Grier. He said you would like it. Do you want to wait for him? Maybe he can join us. Some shuffling noises then Fiona yelped, and Sedotal talked some more. *You don't like hair pulling? Shame. It makes me hot.*

Ty, it doesn't have to be like this. Fiona's voice softened. *I've always liked you. I'll do whatever you want, just let me get cleaned up, okay? You sit down, and I'll be right back.* A long pause, and Grier's heart stopped. *See, baby? We're good. Just let me get ready.* Then came the gunshot.

And the video stopped there. He couldn't even tell if she stopped it or he did. For all Grier knew, he could have been walking into a trap set by his wife and her lover, but he had to believe that Fiona hadn't lied to him, that she genuinely cared for him and complied to save herself and the baby.

He pulled into the driveway and ran up the porch steps to the door, gun in hand.

Sage, beside him, pointed to a droplet of blood on the concrete next to his boot. Grier didn't wait to bust through the door. He couldn't. The wood splintered as he put his shoulder into it. "Fiona!"

Silence.

"Fiona!"

He took the stairs and left Sage on the main floor. He searched every nook, cranny, closet, and cabinet. The entire house was empty except for a circular bloodstain about the size of an orange on the living room carpet and a few droplets leading outside. No other sign of Sedotal or Fiona. Grier couldn't breathe. Literally. Couldn't catch his breath, no matter how hard he gasped, trying. Not even when he bent over and braced his hands on his knees. His lungs didn't work. Nor his heart. Or his brain.

Oh, God. Fiona!

"Grier, she's out here!"

Sage stood at the French doors in her kitchen, yanked one open, and walked outside. Grier, paralyzed, couldn't move, but watched Fiona stand, her white robe dotted with blood. Her eyes were glassy and her cheeks tear-stained, but she made her way inside to him. Not shot. Not dead.

He hugged her, hard, tight, close. "Oh, God, Fi. Are you okay?"

"I shot him, Grier." She held the gun up and waved it at the ceiling.

"I know, baby." Her mouth twisted from one side to the other. She was one tear away from a breakdown. Giving an order was a lot different than doing the job herself. It was the one thing Max hadn't managed to teach her. "It's all right. He deserved it." And if the bastard lived, he would get much worse when Grier got his hands around Sedotal's neck. "Are you okay?"

She didn't look at him "He was going to hurt me."

Grier held her at arm's length intent on checking her for injuries, but he could do that with her wrapped around him. "Babe, are you okay?"

Sage, from behind Fiona, slipped the gun out of her hand then stepped away, leaned his shoulder against the kitchen door frame. She pulled a small device, not much bigger than the tracker he'd shown her, from her robe pocket. "He's been watching us. Together."

Oh, God. This fucking guy was going to die. Maybe tonight if he could bear to leave Fiona. He looked over her head at Sage. "You know where to find him?"

"No idea."

Fiona's eyes cleared. "He said you told him to come." She blinked.

"Fiona, I would never…"

She shook her head. "I want him dead." Now that was a command if he'd ever heard one. Sage, who'd been on the phone, looked at Grier. Grier stared at Fiona for a second, memorizing her face, the fear in her eyes. It would make killing Sedotal easier.

"Ham said to meet him at the clubhouse. He's tossing Sedotal's room." Sage pushed off the wall and made for the door.

"I want you to take her to the hospital and get her checked out. Then stay with her." He tucked his gun in the back waistband of his pants and pulled his shirt over it as he walked to the door. "I'll be back when I find him." And God help the son of a bitch when he did.

19

Unreasonable. The only word Fiona could come up with for her anger. Grier hadn't known Sedotal was insane. Hadn't known he would try to… she couldn't even think past the word. All she knew was that she couldn't think of Grier without her blood curdling in her veins.

And she hadn't seen him either. Not for more than a few minutes in days. That it didn't bother her, bothered her. She needed to go home, clean up the mess she'd made fighting off Sedotal. A fight she should never have been in. And she needed to check for cameras. Sage had found six, but she wanted to check for herself. No telling where else the twisted son of a bitch had hidden them or what he'd seen. Shame brought a new bout of bile to her throat.

She didn't dwell too hard on the fact she'd been the

one to hire him. Or that she hadn't checked him out quite thoroughly enough. Because when she'd had Sage do it, he'd found a dishonorable discharge, a couple of domestic dispute arrests, and an attempted rape. Not that the Screaming Demons were angels. By no means. They had their share of felons, but no rapists or woman beaters.

Grier had told her a hundred times he hated the bastard. Maybe more. And she'd ignored him. Thought he was questioning her judgment. But he should've tried harder to make her listen, pointed out the dangers, or if he'd been so worried, had Sage do the looking before Sedotal ever made it into her house.

And with all the missing shipments, the fire, Hamilton's broken jaw, he should've never sent her home alone without sensing danger. And if something had happened to her baby—hers now, not theirs—Sedotal wouldn't have been the only one needing an undertaker. Assuming Grier ever found him. Which didn't look likely.

"Hey, Fiona." Hamilton stood at the door to her office. For a second, she thought it absurd how little time it had taken her to stop thinking of it as Max's office rather than hers.

"What's up?" The only reason she didn't send him away was because he'd been out with Grier looking for Sedotal and she needed news.

"Have you seen Grier?"

"No." And thank God. She didn't feel like explaining why she had bags four puffs deep under her eyes and why despite being pregnant, she'd lost a couple of pounds. "Why?"

"He looks almost as bad as you do. Thought maybe you could talk to him." He stood and widened his eyes. "But I can see you're probably the wrong person for the job."

On so many levels. "He's a big boy. He can take care of himself."

"Yeah, that's what he said."

Not five minutes after Hamilton left, Jez walked in and plopped into the chair across her desk. "Ham is worried."

Join the club. "He mentioned."

"You been eating? Sleeping?"

"I eat and sleep." Just not very well on either account.

"You're not eating and you're not sleeping and neither is he." She leaned forward and put her elbows on the desk. "You miss him?"

"No." Maybe a little. But more, she remained angry. Hurt.

Jez shook her head. Maybe she could see the tiny part of Fiona that lied. "Fi, you should talk to him." Talk to him. Talk to him. Talk to him. What was she supposed to say to him? Talk about her feelings? Not while she had to work so hard to keep them from bubbling to the surface. *But thank you very much for the advice.*

"We're fine. Just think of us as an old married couple." And thanks to Sedotal's cameras, everyone probably already knew what was or wasn't between her and Grier. *An old married couple with no secrets.*

"One on the verge of divorce maybe."

Divorce. Had he mentioned divorce? Fiona couldn't think about it.

"Enough, okay." Aside from not wanting to hear anymore, she just didn't feel like hashing it out with anyone. Grier included.

Jez stood. "You're gonna mess around and lose him." At the door she stopped. "And you won't have anyone to blame but yourself."

Not the news flash Jez seemed to think. Also not newsworthy enough for Fiona to care to take action. She had a desk full of obligations. Grier could handle his, and she would handle hers.

She earned a five-minute reprieve before the man himself walked into her office and occupied her very popular today chair. Her head ached and Hamilton and Jez had already worn her patience thin. Not likely that in her mood, Grier could make it any better. But she tossed her pen onto the desk and sat back, fingers laced in her lap.

The old tingle vibrated through her, not as intense as before, but still there. She would have been annoyed, but it came with memories she couldn't find it in herself to be bitter about.

"Hey."

"Hi." He didn't look good. He needed a few weeks of sleep, a shave, maybe something warm to eat. They stayed silent staring at one another until finally, she looked away. "Grier, I have a lot to do."

He nodded but remained seated. "You feeling okay?"

No. And she couldn't quite figure out what exactly she could do to feel better, but sitting here, in this room, staring at him damned sure didn't offer any relief. "I'm fine."

To his credit, he didn't scoff. Only smiled. "Me, too." Fiona couldn't tell which was thicker—the tension or the awkwardness between them. "Bunch of worriers out there." He jerked his thumb toward the door.

She nodded. "Yeah."

"Maybe we should talk. We haven't really..." He cleared his throat. "Had much time since..."

She didn't want or need to talk. "It happened. It's done. And I'm not worried about Sedotal or anyone getting to me. Hamilton has been staying in one of the rooms here so I'm safe."

"Meaning you weren't safe with me?" A flicker of hurt flashed in his eyes.

She didn't answer, partly because she didn't know what to say and partly because there wasn't any point in starting a big fight. She just didn't have one left in her.

"Look, Grier. I'm pregnant. If I look like crap"—which she did, although he'd never say—"it's because I have a human growing inside me. It's a little disorienting for my body. It doesn't have anything to do with you or Tyler Sedotal or anything else."

His mouth twitched. "Well, I look like shit because another man is protecting my wife when it should be me." He sighed. "And it's killing me."

If he kept saying things like that, she would fall apart. She had to stay angry to keep the rest of her emotions quiet. At least until she could get her head straight, stop dreaming about Sedotal touching her, the kiss she'd been forced to give him, the gunshot she heard even when awake and that damned tattoo of his that looked more like a brand than ink.

"Grier, can we do this later? I have so much work. I have to figure out how to keep customers and… write checks…" She picked up a stack of unopened envelopes. "Days and days worth of mail to go through."

"Tonight then?"

"Aren't you still watching the shipments?" She'd specifically told Hamilton she wanted Grier on them.

"It's taken care of."

Again, no point in arguing. She nodded. "I guess we'll see." She could have been talking about the shipments or them.

He didn't ask, and she didn't elaborate. And for the first time since she'd known him, she didn't watch him walk away, even though she appreciated the view more than most others she'd ever seen. She had enough memories of him walking away. Adding another to her reserve would have just been overkill.

She leaned back in her seat and spun toward the wall. It just wouldn't do for anyone else to walk in and find her crying.

Fucking Sedotal. Every day that passed reinforced Grier's hatred. Made him want to tear the son of a bitch apart. For what he'd done to Fiona and what he'd done to them as a couple. Fiona wouldn't even look at him, and the few times she did, he could see the blame in her eyes.

Justifiable blame. He never should have sent her home alone. Whenever he thought about what could have happened, how she'd trembled when he'd gotten there, the manic eyes and waving gun, his anger went wild. Uncontrollable. And Sedotal had disappeared. Like he'd never even existed.

Grier and Sage had followed every lead, even talking to some of the guys he'd been in the military with. Somehow, the guy had gone ghost. And he couldn't tell Fiona that he'd failed her again, so he continued to look. Every free minute of the day and night, he drove around searching up and down the east coast. He'd planned another search for tonight, but he wasn't getting anywhere anyway and talking to Fiona held a place of equal prominence on the totem pole of his life.

He walked to the bar and sat heavily on the stool. The weight of the world curved his back. Sage slapped him on the shoulder. "Still not talking to you, huh?"

Jesus, did everybody know everything about their relationship? Grier shook his head and took a beer from Jez.

"Give her some time. She'll come around."

Grier didn't point out the flaw in Jez's words of wisdom. Fiona didn't want to talk to him and no amount of time would change it. And she shouldn't want to talk to her. He'd let her down, let Max down, let himself down.

He turned to Sage. "I'm going to hang around here tonight. Would you mind…?"

"Yeah. No problem. I'll take Frank. Maybe you can get some sleep."

He doubted it, but maybe. If Fiona talked to him, they could figure this out. This being their situation and how to fix all the things wrong between them. He hadn't had her long but the thought of losing her now stole his breath. And his courage. And his reason for getting up in the morning. He would tell her he loved her. He had to. If she walked away, and after he told her, he would offer her the opportunity, then at least she would know exactly who and what she was walking away from. But God, he hoped she stayed. Or let him stay.

Fatigue like he'd never known before made his eyes heavy, but he didn't have much hope for sleep. Like every night as soon as he put head to pillow, his brain taunted him, teased him with all the ways he'd messed up and fantasy images of the family slipping through his fingers. Besides, he needed to take the tracking device to the supplier if he wasn't going to be there.

He didn't know how many of the guys knew he still used the app to track the shipments since they hadn't been hit in a while and he'd stopped talking much to Sage—top-secret meant top-secret—but he didn't want to take any chances. And since he wouldn't be there tonight, he wanted to make damned sure he could find that truck if it somehow disappeared.

Leaving the almost full beer on top of the bar, he looked at Sage. "I need to go clear my head. I'll be back."

"Want some company?"

"Nah. I just need some time."

Even when he was young and full of confidence and plenty of arrogance, riding had always been his go-to for deep thinking, though he didn't know how he'd manage thinking at all with his mind so cluttered. If nothing else, at least he'd be away from all the stares and concern at the clubhouse. And maybe even as much as thinking it out, he needed to be away from them.

SINCE HE'D COME BACK LATER than he'd expected, sidetracked by something he couldn't get out of, Grier checked all the spare rooms at the clubhouse for Fiona. When he didn't find her, he went back to the bar. "Where's Fiona?"

Lisa smiled. "She tore out of here this afternoon with Sage. Haven't seen either one of them since."

"All right." But goddammit, it wasn't all right. He needed to see her. Needed to hold her, apologize, do whatever it took to make this right. He couldn't consider another outcome. Not now.

He went to the back and found the room she'd been staying in. A nap until she got back wouldn't hurt. He laid down on the bed, turned his face into the pillow and inhaled the sweet, fresh scent of Fiona. For the first time in days or weeks or maybe years, sleep came easily.

20

Fiona stared at the photo. Grainy at best. Could have been photoshopped. She couldn't tell. Distance and shadows played games with her eyes. But Ralph would know. Ralph was the master of photo manipulation, and her father had used him more than once to sway certain political and authoritative figures to the side which most benefited Demon business.

He held the picture in his hand and studied the finer points of the image, turning it, holding it up to the light. He even walked out of the office with it to stand on the sidewalk and let the sun reveal whatever mysteries it held. He walked back inside and around to his desk then pulled out a magnifying glass to further his study.

She didn't really care what he had to do. She needed

to know—and in her heart she did—whether or not this damned thing was real.

Fiona stood behind him in his cramped office that only fit his desk—a scarred wood that despite being old would never be classified as an antique—and a chair of equal age with bright orange vinyl armrests and seat cushion. She leaned over his back, trying to see what he saw until he set the magnifier down perfectly perpendicular to his desk blotter. "Do you mind? You're fogging up my lens with your hot lady breath."

Yes, she did mind, but Fiona moved to the lone chair on the other side of the desk. Sage stood at the door, arms and ankles crossed, head down as if the pattern in the carpet intrigued him. "Is it real?"

He sighed. His bald head shined under the overhead lights and the age spots in his hands wobbled when he reached for his paper coffee cup. He held it out to her. "Why don't you go out and get a cup of coffee. Come back in a half-hour. I'll know more by then."

Translation: he wanted her gone. But she hadn't made a copy of the picture, and damned if she intended to let the original out of her sight. She shook her head, but Sage stood. "Come on, Fiona. Let's let him work. You want him to get it right."

She scowled at Sage then at Ralph but stood. "We'll be right outside."

Her stomach clenched. She needed definitive proof.

Really needed to know if her husband had betrayed the club. Again. She didn't want the picture to be an authentic one or to believe Grier would risk hurting their baby or her. She wanted it to be a phony, to know that someone had put Grier's head on a different body. Then the envelope or whatever it had inside wouldn't matter. But part of her knew it was him. Not even the part that was all anger and red-hazed glares. It was the part of her that knew him intimately, recognized the curve of his ass, the breadth of his shoulders.

That he was handing an envelope—what else would it be but money—to the now-dead driver of the burned shipment meant she'd found her traitor. She'd been happy to blame Sedotal until she'd found a large, brown, unmarked envelope on her desk. Her world, already teetering, crashed down in front of her when she pulled out this goddamned picture.

Sage led her all the way to the sidewalk. She clasped her shaking hands. This was too much. Singularly, she could handle any one of the issues on her pile, but it was a pile now. A big, dirty pile of secrets, lies, and pain so raw she could barely find it in herself to crawl out of bed in the morning. And only one thing she could say for certain. If this picture proved to be true, she wouldn't lie for Grier a second time.

And they would kill him.

As if Sage could read her mind, he dropped a hand

on her shoulder. "He might have an explanation. It could be… nothing."

But his words didn't hide his doubt. "Thanks for bringing me. I know you guys are tight…"

Sage nodded. "You want a coffee or something?" He pointed to the coffee shop. "Maybe a donut for the little guy?"

She couldn't remember the last time she'd eaten or even been interested in food. "Yeah. That sounds good."

He walked away, and she tapped her foot against the sidewalk. Maybe there was an explanation. Not that she could think of one. Not that it would make a difference. She turned to look into the window, didn't notice the man behind her until he put his hand on her shoulder. "Hey, Fi."

"Grier." If she tried hard enough, closed her eyes, and listened with her heart instead of her head, she could almost pretend things hadn't changed between them. She smiled. Wishing. Hoping. Then she turned, and all her hope died away.

"What are you doing standing out here on the sidewalk?"

"Sage went to get us coffee." She didn't have a reason to be outside Ralph's office. "What are you doing here?"

"Heard you went to see Ralph." He moved to stand next to her, and they both faced the street. "You stood me up last night."

"Oh. Yeah." She'd found him in her bed at the club-house and stayed with Jez. After finding the picture, she just couldn't face him. "I, um, uh…"

"Am avoiding me."

She nodded. "Yeah." She shook her head. "Grier, I can't do the big 'us' talk. Not now. There's too much going on." She didn't look at him. Wouldn't survive looking into the face of his hurt or anger or anything else there.

"Fiona." He ducked his head. "I know you're angry that I didn't protect you." When he brushed her hair back and tucked it behind her ear then left his hand at her cheek, she almost melted. For one second. Then her anger came right back.

"Grier. I can't…"

He sighed. "Please, Fiona. I just need to say some things." He didn't speak again until she nodded. "You're right. I should've taken better care of you. You're my family. You and the baby. But I won't ever make that mistake again." He pushed off the wall. "I just wanted you to know that." He started to walk away then turned and came back. "And that I love you." He pulled her in and brushed his lips over her hair then walked away again. And this time, she watched him go.

Fiona stared at Ralph. "What the hell does that mean?" An entire day—felt like it anyway—she'd waited for something that would tilt her decision to the right side. She'd drank enough decaf her stomach sloshed and she'd peed about twenty-five times. And if she'd heard him right, Ralph had nothing.

"It means this is a picture that may or may not have been tampered with. It's not an original print either way. And *that* means unless you find the original, I won't be much help."

She'd been here three hours already. Wasted time. "Are you sure? There's no way you can tell?" With as much as her father had paid him over the years, he should have been able to afford not only a nicer office but some serious FBI kind of equipment.

"I'm sorry, Fiona."

She blew her breath out and stood, holding out her hand for the photo. "Thanks, Ralph." She smiled and slid the picture back into the envelope.

"If you find the original, you probably won't need me, but if you do, just call. I'm here for you, always." Her dad's name carried an expected weight. Always had. She hadn't needed to make an appointment even. When she arrived, Ralph flipped his sign to closed and only worked on the photo. He was a good man who didn't mind the shadiness of her father's business, and he did a good job, had proven his loyalty to the Demons over and over again. She would continue their working relationship whether she found the photo or not.

Sage led her outside. "I saw Grier."

"Yeah, so did I."

"Did you tell him about the picture?" Sage had lobbied for her to just ask him all the way from the clubhouse to Ralph's office as he'd sat in the passenger seat staring at the image of Grier.

She shook her head. "Did you?"

"No. And I won't if you don't want me to." He wouldn't. She trusted him. Of course, she'd trusted Grier, too, and now... she felt like a fool charmed by the local conman. She just didn't know his con yet.

"What do I do, Sage?" She covered her face with the envelope then fanned herself with it. "I mean, he's my husband. I should trust him. I shouldn't be running around, wasting my day, trying to prove him good or bad. I should know it." Not that she could honestly say she would mind bad, but in this circumstance, she wanted him to be good.

"You could just..." He shook his head and shrugged. "Ask him. Show him the picture and tell him you need to know."

That wouldn't work. "He's too good. I can't tell when he's lying."

"Has he lied to you?" God. She wanted to tell someone what he'd asked her to do and that she'd done it. But she couldn't. The guys knowing she had put Grier first, in front of her duty to the club would ruin everything she'd worked for, everything her dad had spent his life building.

And besides that one time, she couldn't think of another where he'd told her a lie. "No."

"Then ask him, Fiona. Unless you can figure out where that picture came from and how to get the original." He opened the door to her father's Mercedes. She'd been driving all of her father's cars to see which one she wanted to keep.

On the way back to the clubhouse, Sage drove slowly, as if he had no idea how to operate a vehicle with more than two wheels. They were beeped at, flipped off, passed on the right and left, and still, Sage kept his hands at ten and two and the speed at a rip-roaring twenty-five.

Finally, he pulled into the lot, and she watched him wipe the sweat from above his lip. "Thank God."

"Do you not like driving cars?"

"Not an eighty-thousand-dollar car that belonged to Max. I wreck that thing, he'd probably haunt me." He dropped the key fob into her palm.

She smiled, a genuine one and her first in what felt like years. "Probably."

Before he opened the door, he turned in the seat to look at her. "You know what? Max trusted Grier with the person he loved most in his life. And I've never met a better judge of character before in my life than Max. Maybe… think about that."

Sage didn't know Grier had run off with Kye and Eliana. "Sage…"

"When he came back and you gave us that story about business abroad. Come on, Fiona." He shook his head. "Nobody was buying that. What does a motorcycle club that bootlegs hot motorcycle parts and dabbles in drugs and money have to do abroad? We're local. And good at it, no doubt, but we aren't quite at an international level, right?" She sighed. No point in confirming what he already knew. "He came back, and Max let him. That says something about both of them."

She smiled. "Goddammit, Sage. I was ready to hate him."

"Yeah, but what would your dad say?" He returned her grin.

What would her dad say? Maybe Sage was right. Time to think like Max. Or at least to use everything he gave her to make the decisions she knew she had to make. She was strong enough to do this. Or Max would have chosen someone else to run this club. He'd chosen her because she was strong. Now, it was time to prove it.

* * *

GRIER STARED from the photo to the firm line of Fiona's lips and back to the photo. He sat in the chair, and she stood, legs and arms crossed in a hands-off pose just to his left with her hip resting against the desk. Her perfume tingled in his nose and his hands itched to touch her, but he stared at the picture instead. The fucking picture.

"Is it you?" He'd never heard her voice so hard.

He nodded. "Yeah." No point in lying. This was a picture worth zero words since he couldn't talk about it. And what horrible timing for it to appear. For God's sake. She'd been at Ralph's to verify its authenticity. So she already knew.

She pointed to the driver. "The other guy… Dave… had four kids. His wife, Melanie, had to identify his body." Fiona didn't stammer or stutter. Her voice held strength and anger. Neither boded well for Grier. "I held her hand and promised I would find whoever did this to him." She blew out a breath not nearly as unaffected as she wanted him to believe.

"Fiona… I can explain."

"Is this picture and what you're doing in it the reason Dave is gone?"

No. But Grier couldn't tell the truth. It looked as bad as if he was the one who'd gotten Dave killed. And while he'd said he could explain, he lied. At least not without putting Dave's family at risk. He had no idea such a picture existed. Or who would've taken it. "Yeah." The only thing Grier knew for sure was that he would take this secret with him to his grave no matter what. Dave's family deserved that. On the bright side, it looked like that would be sooner than he thought. And at least then he wouldn't have to tell Fiona.

DARK DESIRES
~ A billionaire dark romance series ~
Dark Desire
Dark Rules
Dark Secret
Dark Time
Dark Truth

BARRE TO BAR
~ A billionaire second chance series ~
Dancing With Lies
Dancing With Temptation
Dancing With Doubt
Dancing With Guilt
Dancing With Redemption

TWISTED INTENTION

~ A billionaire revenge romance series ~

Twisted Beauty

Twisted Love

Twisted Fate

Mafia's Obsession

~ A hot mafia romance series ~

Mafia's Dirty Secret

Mafia's Fake Bride

Mafia's Final Play

Screaming Demons

~ An MC romance series full of suspense ~

Rough Start

Rough Ride

Rough Choice

Rough Patch

Rough Return

Rough Road

Rough Trip

Rough Night

Rough Love

Standalone Contemporary Romance

Billionaire in Vegas

Billionaire Hunt

Billionaire's Game
Billionaire Retreat
Billionaire On Air
A Chance To Love
Somebody To Love
Not Mine To Love

Check out Summer's entire collection at
www.summercooper.com/books

ABOUT SUMMER COOPER

Thank you so much for reading. Without you, it wouldn't be possible for me to be a full-time author. I hope you enjoy reading my books as much as I do writing them.

Besides (obviously!) reading and writing, I also love cuddling my dogs, shouting at Alexa, being upside down (aka Yoga) and driving my family cray-cray!

Get in touch at
hello@summercooper.com
www.summercooper.com

facebook.com/summercooperauthor
instagram.com/summercooperauthor
goodreads.com/summercooper
bookbub.com/profile/summer-cooper